Nikos walked away from the door, dazed.

He paced down the corridor and back again, one word circling through his mind: *father.*

His only association with the concept of fatherhood was a toxic and complicated matter. His own father had been many things, but a father in the true sense of the word hadn't been one of them. Nikos didn't even know what having a father felt like.

He reeled as the significance of this sank in.

If it was true.

One minute he'd had his hands full of Maggie, feverish with lust, her curves even more delicious than he remembered, and the next he'd been looking at a baby in her arms.

He was back outside the bedroom door now. He could hear Maggie's voice, indistinct, making crooning noises.

Nikos looked around. Nothing but an empty corridor and the woman behind this door with a baby who might or might not be his. And what had she said? Something about "you know you are"? That made no sense to him at all.

The Marchetti Dynasty

They live a superrich lifestyle—but for this dynasty to survive, these brothers need brides!

The Marchetti name is synonymous with luxury—their family business boasts the most opulent brands from fashion to real estate. While the three Marchetti brothers live a superrich existence and have no trouble attracting women, they know little about love. They have even less in common! Now they are going to have to work together to protect their inheritance—and securing the Marchetti dynasty will mean learning that gaining wives and heirs is going to take far more than a little seduction!

Meet the Marchetti brothers and the feisty and resourceful women who tame them in:

Nikos and Maggie's story:
The Maid's Best Kept Secret

Available now

And look out for

Maks and Zoe's story

Sharif and Aliyah's story

Coming soon

Abby Green

THE MAID'S BEST KEPT SECRET

HARLEQUIN
PRESENTS

Recycling programs for this product may not exist in your area.

ISBN-13: 978-1-335-89389-5

The Maid's Best Kept Secret

This edition published by arrangement with Harlequin Books S.A.

For questions and comments about the quality of this book, please contact us at CustomerService@Harlequin.com.

Harlequin Enterprises ULC
22 Adelaide St. West, 40th Floor
Toronto, Ontario M5H 4E3, Canada
www.Harlequin.com

Printed in U.S.A.

Irish author **Abby Green** ended a very glamorous career in film and TV—which really consisted of a lot of standing in the rain outside actors' trailers—to pursue her love of romance. After she'd bombarded Harlequin with manuscripts they kindly accepted one, and an author was born. She lives in Dublin, Ireland, and loves any excuse for distraction. Visit abby-green.com or email abbygreenauthor@gmail.com.

Books by Abby Green

Harlequin Presents

The Virgin's Debt to Pay
Awakened by the Scarred Italian
The Greek's Unknown Bride

Conveniently Wed!

Claiming His Wedding Night Consequence

One Night With Consequences

An Innocent, A Seduction, A Secret

Rival Spanish Brothers

Confessions of a Pregnant Cinderella
Redeemed by His Stolen Bride

Rulers of the Desert

A Diamond for the Sheikh's Mistress
A Christmas Bride for the King

Visit the Author Profile page
at Harlequin.com for more titles.

This is my fiftieth title for Harlequin and it's beyond shocking to write that down, let alone contemplate how it happened over the last thirteen years.

I'd like to dedicate this book first and foremost to my mother, without whom I wouldn't have inherited a love of reading, writing and a very dark sense of humor.

To my writer tribe: Heidi, Iona, Fiona, Susan and Sharon. Without you all, the writing world would be far duller and scarier to navigate. (And Carol Marinelli—sounding board and car enabler.)

To the McDermot and Mernagh clan, who adopted me into their family a long time ago before any of us knew how much I would need them.

To Susie Q, Eoin, Lucy, Lynn, Lorna, Lindi and Ruth, who encouraged me to take the leap into a new world.

To Hazel, who provides daily sustenance, free therapy and MUK online updates.

To Gervaise Landy, who planted the seed (and had "that tape") that led to me writing a Harlequin book in the very first instance.

To my Harlequin editors, who have guided me and continue to guide me along the way: Tessa Shapcott, Katinka Proudfoot, Meg Lewis, Suzy Clarke and Sheila Hodgson. Without editors, writers are nothing.

And last but not least, to you, lovely romance readers. I, too, am a romance reader and so we're all in on the secret: that the romance genre simply is the best.

As long as people want to hear or read stories, they will want romance, because love—in all its myriad shapes and forms—is the most important thing.

CHAPTER ONE

MAGGIE TAGGART FELT RESTLESS. She'd finished washing up the dishes in the sink and looked around the vast and gleaming kitchen which was situated in the basement of an even vaster house. A stunningly beautiful period country house, to be exact. Set in some ten acres of lush green land about an hour's drive outside Dublin.

There were manicured gardens to the rear and a sizeable walled kitchen garden to the side. There was even a small lake and a forest. And stables. But the stables were empty. The owner— a billionaire tycoon—had apparently bought the house sight unseen on a whim when he'd had a passing interest in investing in horse racing, for which this part of Ireland was renowned.

Except he'd never bought any horses and he'd never actually visited the house. So here it sat, empty and untouched. Luxuriously decorated to his specifications. He hadn't even hired the housekeeper himself—one of his assistants had done it remotely.

That housekeeper had been Maggie's mother, and when she'd fallen ill she had been terrified of losing her job. So Maggie had quit her own job as a commis chef in a Dublin restaurant and come to help her and take care of her. Leaving her restaurant job hadn't been too much of a sacrifice, thanks to the head chef, who had been a serial groper of his female staff.

Then Maggie's mother had died suddenly, and when she'd informed the owner's offices an impersonal assistant had asked if she wouldn't mind taking over in the interim, while they found a permanent replacement.

Maggie had been in shock…grieving…so she'd found herself saying yes, relishing the thought of a quiet space where she could lick her wounds and deal with her grief, not yet ready to face back into the world.

That had been three months ago. Three months that had passed in a grief-stricken blur. And she was only just emerging from that very intial painful stage.

Hence this sense of restlessness. Up to now the house had served as a kind of cocoon, shielding her from the outside world. But she could feel herself itching to do more than just tend to it. In spite of its lack of occupants, it was surprisingly challenging to maintain at the high standard demanded by the boss—should he ever decide to drop by. On another whim.

Maggie's soft mouth firmed. The impression she had of the owner—a man she wasn't interested enough in to look up on the internet—was one of gross entitlement. Who bought a lavish country house and then never even came to see it?

'Rich, powerful men who have more money than sense.'

Those had been her mother's words. And she had known all about rich, powerful men—because Maggie's father had been one. A wealthy property tycoon from Scotland, he'd had an affair with Maggie's mother and when she'd told him she was pregnant he'd denied all knowledge, terrified that Maggie's mother and his illegitimate daughter might get their hands on his vast fortune.

He hadn't offered any support or commitment. He'd offered only threats and intimidation. Maggie's mother had been too proud and heartbroken to pursue him for maintenance and they'd left Scotland and moved to Ireland, where Maggie's mother's job as a housekeeper had kept them moving around the country, never really settling in any one place for long.

To say that Maggie had a jaded view of rich men and their ways was an understatement. She sighed. However, she was being paid very generously to take care of an empty house by a rich man, so she couldn't really complain.

At that moment the peace that she'd so relished

was shattered by a sound from upstairs—the ground floor. A banging noise. The front door? It was such an unusual sound to hear in this silent house that she almost didn't recognise it.

Maggie rushed upstairs and walked into the hall just as the knocker was slammed down onto the door again. She muttered, 'Keep your hair on…' as she switched on the outside light and swung the door open.

And promptly ceased breathing at the sight in front of her. A tall, dark man dominated the doorway, hand lifted as if to slam the knocker down again. His other arm was raised, and rested on the door frame. The late-summer sky was a dusky lavender behind him, making him seem even darker.

Maggie couldn't find her breath. Dressed in a classic black tuxedo, he was the most stupendously gorgeous man she'd ever seen. Thick curly hair and dark brows framed a strong-boned face…cheekbones to die for. His deep-set eyes were dark, but not brown. Golden. His skin was dark too. There was stubble on his jaw. The sheer height, width and breadth of him was heat-inducingly powerful.

She registered all this in a split-second—a very basic biological reaction to a virile male.

His black bowtie hung rakishly undone under the open top button of his shirt. Those dark eyes flicked down from her face over her body. A bold appraisal. Arrogant, even.

Maggie became acutely aware of the fact that she was wearing cut-off shorts and a sleeveless T-shirt, her hair up in an untidy bun. Her habitual uniform for when she was cleaning.

'This *is* Kildare House?' the masculine vision asked, with a slight accent.

His voice was deep and rough and the pulse between her legs throbbed. Most disturbing.

'Yes, it is.'

The man stood up straight. He had an air of slightly louche inebriation but his eyes were too focused and direct for him to be intoxicated. Actually, it was an air of intense ennui.

He turned away from her, and it was only then that Maggie noticed a taxi at the bottom of the steps leading up to the front door, engine idling.

The man addressed the driver, who was waiting by the car. 'This is the right place. Thank you.'

Maggie watched with growing shock as the taxi driver waved jauntily, got into his car and drove off.

She gripped the door. 'Excuse me but who *are* you?'

The man turned back to face her. 'I'm the owner of this house. Nikos Marchetti, I think the more pertinent question here is who are *you*?

Because I've seen a picture of the housekeeper and you are most definitely not her.'

Nikos Marchetti. The owner she'd envisaged as middle-aged, paunchy, entitled. But this man was more like a Spartan warrior, sheathed in the modern-day trappings of a suit.

His eyes were dropping down her body again, with that insolent appraisal that should have disgusted Maggie but which was having an altogether far less acceptable effect on her body.

She drew herself up to her full five foot ten inches and crossed her arms over her chest. So far Nikos Marchetti was doing little *not* to live up to what she'd expected. Behaviourally, if not physically.

'I am Maggie Taggart—Edith's daughter. She died three months ago and your staff asked if I'd stay on until another housekeeper was hired. Something you're evidently not aware of.'

He looked at her, expressionless. 'I most likely wasn't informed. My staff are briefed not to bother me unless it's something urgent, and clearly they felt that you could handle the job. However, I am sorry for your loss. Do you think I could enter my own property now?'

His casual dismissal and tacked-on condolences for one of the most traumatic events in Maggie's life—losing her beloved mother—made her stand her ground. 'How do I know you are who you say you are? You could be anyone.'

* * *

Nikos Marchetti looked at the woman in front of him and felt not a little shock and surprise running through his system. Along with something much more potent—the biggest jolt of insta-lust he'd ever felt in his life.

He'd just come from a black-tie event at Dublin Castle—leaving behind a room heaving with some of the most beautiful women in the world. And not one of them had turned his head like this…this fiery sprite.

Except she was too tall to be a sprite. She was strong. Supple. The full breasts evident under her thin T-shirt left little to the imagination, and she had wide hips and long pale legs that went on for ever. She was like a Viking queen—all woman and perfectly, generously proportioned—and Nikos's brain was melting into a heat haze.

Which was probably why he was still standing there, long past the time he would normally have indulged such impertinence.

It wasn't just her body, though. Unruly-looking red-gold hair was pulled up into a bun on top of her head and her bone structure was exquisite—high cheekbones, firm jaw, straight nose. Her face was dominated by huge blue eyes and a wide, generous mouth. Currently tight. Like the arms across her chest, blocking him from entering his own property.

'You've never even been here before, have you?'

Nikos arched a brow. 'I wasn't aware I had to account to you for my movements—but, no, I haven't been here before.'

'Why now? Tonight? No one warned me you were coming.'

'As I own the property, and it should be in a state of readiness for my arrival at any time, I didn't see the need to forewarn or inform anyone,' Nikos drawled.

'It's late... I could have been in bed.'

Nikos was rewarded with a very unhelpful image of this woman lying back on a bed naked, hair spread around her head, welcoming him to explore her sensual body. Blood rushed to his already heated groin, making him hard—something he was usually much more in control of.

Now irritation prickled. 'Seriously? You're denying me entry?'

'I am until you show me some identification. If you are who you say you are, then surely you can appreciate the fact that I'm not going to let a stranger into your property?'

Nikos wanted to growl. There were very few instances when he wasn't automatically obeyed. Except she had a point. The fact that she apparently didn't recognise him was also a novelty that had an unexpected appeal. He was used to people targeting him because of exactly who he was: heir to a vast inestimable fortune and legacy.

But he didn't want to think about that now—

it would only remind him of the feeling of ennui and claustrophobia that had driven him here in the first place, even though he'd almost forgotten about the Irish estate he owned.

He dug into his inside pocket and muttered, 'I can't believe I'm doing this…' before pulling out his passport and handing it to his housekeeper.

Who looked more like a cheerleader, with that supple body and fresh-faced beauty.

Before he could censor himself he said, 'How old are you?'

She looked up from the passport. 'Twenty-three. This is a Greek passport. I thought you were Italian?'

Nikos took the passport back. 'I'm half-Greek, half-Italian and I decided to go with my Greek side. Any more questions? Or can I now enter the property I own?'

Maggie couldn't believe she was being so antagonistic to the owner of this house. Because he *was* the owner.

Nikos Marchetti.

She scrabbled to recall the vague information she'd absorbed from her mother about him, but her mother's illness had taken most of her attention. He was heir to a vast fortune—the Marchetti Group. But even she knew who *they* were. The biggest conglomerate of luxury brands in the world. They also owned vast swathes of real estate—hotels, nightclubs, and entire blocks in places like New York.

Maggie stood back and moved aside. 'Please, come in, Mr Marchetti. It's a pleasure to welcome you to Kildare House.'

He made a rude sound and walked in, placing a small holdall bag down on a nearby chair. He was even bigger and more gorgeous under the bright lighting of the hallway. He looked around the hall and then proceeded to walk into one of the nearby reception rooms.

Maggie was still reeling from his scent, which had washed over her as he'd entered. Nothing manufactured—or maybe it was just expensive enough not to smell synthetic. Musky, woodsy and pure male essence…

She closed the front door and followed him to the doorway of the reception room to see that he had taken off his jacket and flung it carelessly over the back of a chair. He was at the drinks cabinet and opening a whiskey bottle, pouring a measure into a small tumbler glass.

'Would you like me to show you around?' Maggie asked, aiming to sound professional and breezy when she felt anything but.

Whatever it was about this man, he'd lodged himself under her skin and she prickled all over. With awareness and something much more volatile.

He turned around. 'Sure.'

He walked towards her, taking a sip of the whiskey and keeping the glass in his hand. He looked thoroughly dangerous and disreputable and a little shiver raced over Maggie's skin.

Acutely aware of him, prowling behind her like a large, sensual jungle cat, she showed him the rooms leading off the circular hallway—more reception rooms, formal and informal, and a formal living room. At the back, overlooking the gardens, was a study, filled with state-of-the-art computers which had never been touched.

On the other side of the hall was a less formal living room, complete with media centre and projection screen for watching movies. It was possibly Maggie's favourite room in the house. Floor-to-ceiling shelves full of books lined the walls. Books that she'd surmised had been chosen purely for show. The works of Shakespeare... Dickens...

Nikos Marchetti faced her. 'Lead on.'

Maggie all but tripped over her own feet as she led him back through the hallway and downstairs to the kitchen. He barely glanced at that, clearly more interested in the gym and indoor lap pool on the same level. There were also rooms for massage or spa treatments. A sauna and a steam room.

He couldn't have looked more insouciant, with his open shirt, dangling bowtie and the glass of whiskey in hand, inspecting a property he owned but had never even laid eyes on before. So far every judgement Maggie had ever made about rich, powerful men was being proved right.

He turned to face her and drained his glass, holding it carelessly between two fingers. Was it her imagination or did something in those mesmerising gold eyes flare for a second? She realised now that they weren't entirely golden, there were green flecks too. And hazel.

To her shame and disgust, she felt a wave of heat rise up through her body from her core, and she turned quickly before it could reach her face. As pale as she was, every passing emotion registered on her skin—much to her embarrassment.

'The bedrooms are on the first floor.' Maggie led the way back up to the main area of the house, not even checking to see if Nikos Marchetti was following her.

But he was. She could sense him—as if from the moment she'd seen him, she'd been plugged into a new awareness.

Nikos was finding it hard to notice much about the house when the tantalising vision of his housekeeper's bottom and swaying hips filled his vision as she climbed the stairs in front of him. Not to mention those long bare legs.

Theos. He was usually far more sophisticated than this. He just hadn't expected...*her* to answer the door of his country house in the middle of nowhere outside Dublin.

She was walking briskly down the corridor ahead of him now, opening doors and saying, 'These are all spare bedroom suites. Yours is here at the end…'

She'd opened a door and was standing back. He noticed now that she was wearing flip-flops. And that she had pretty feet. Toenails painted a coral colour.

He gritted his jaw and went into the room—but not before he caught her scent again: crushed roses and something much earthier. Musky. It made him grit his jaw even harder.

He barely took in the luxurious room, with windows overlooking three sides of the house, its gardens barely visible now in the rapidly gathering night. He recognised it from the photos he'd been sent by the interior designer after it had been completed.

This was the first house he'd bought—his other properties were apartments in the hotels his company owned. And now he was here he felt a little exposed—as if his motives for buying the house on the basis of a picture that had caught at his gut were being laid bare for this stranger to see.

He could feel her watching him. This woman with a body built like a siren and those huge blue eyes.

He turned around. Maggie Taggart's arms were

folded across her chest again, which only pushed the generous swells of her breasts together under the thin material of her T-shirt.

The feeling of exposure was not welcome. Nikos didn't *do* introspection.

He deflected the attention back to her. 'Why are you dressed as if you're attending a barbecue?'

Her cheeks flushed. 'If I had been informed of your arrival you can be sure I would have dressed appropriately. However, considering the fact that it's well past official hours, I don't see why I have to justify dressing as I please. In light of the fact that your presence here is somewhat…irregular, I've taken the liberty of working the hours that suit me. I don't think you can fault the state of the house. I work seven days a week and it has been kept in a permanent state of readiness for your arrival.'

Nikos felt his conscience prick. Which was rare for him.

An innate sense of fairness made him admit, 'You *have* kept the house pristine. Look, can we start over?'

He walked over to where she stood in the doorway. Suddenly she didn't look so confident. He could see a pulse throbbing in her neck. *Not as spiky as she looked. Or behaved.*

He held out his hand. 'I'm Nikos Marchetti— owner of this house. Sorry for the lack of notice about my arrival and thank you for keeping it so beautifully. Clearly you are doing an amazing job.'

He congratulated himself on keeping any mocking tone out of his voice.

His housekeeper looked at him suspiciously, but eventually she slipped her hand into his. Immediately Nikos felt the slightly rough skin of her palm, and the desire he felt turned into full-on arousal. Hot and pulsing through every vein. Instinctively he closed his hand around hers.

Maggie couldn't breathe again. What had this man just said? Her brain felt fuzzy. All she was aware of was how big his hand felt around hers, dwarfing it completely. Dwarfing *her*, actually. She was tall, and she'd got used to being described by various people throughout her life as *a big, strong girl*, but Nikos Marchetti towered over her, and for the first time in her life she felt…delicate.

Even in heels she'd barely graze his jaw—a fact which, though she hated to admit it, was a little intoxicating. It was rare for her to have to look up at a man. Not that she'd ever had much opportunity. A lifetime of moving around with her mother hadn't been conducive to forming a core group of close friends, and the few dates she'd embarked upon in a bid to broaden her social circle had invariably ended with a limp handshake when the men had turned out to be several inches smaller than her. Every single time.

So for that and a myriad other reasons—including her general mistrust of men, bred into her by her mother—she'd shied away from intimacy. But here…now…it felt very intimate.

She pulled her hand free. 'Have you eaten this evening? There's some leftover chicken stew. I can't remember if it's on your list of preferred foods, but you're welcome to some if you'd like me to heat it up?'

She was babbling—a habit when she was nervous and one she hated. She took a few steps back, putting some much-needed space between her and this man who was making her think about all sorts of things and…*intimacy.* He was her boss.

He shrugged minutely. 'Sure. I need to take a shower and change. I'll be down shortly.'

Maggie said, 'Your walk-in dressing room is stocked with a full wardrobe, should you need anything.'

She went downstairs and cursed herself for being so affected by him. He was undeniably gorgeous and sexy, yes, but he probably had the same effect on everyone he encountered. It was just proof that she wasn't immune to his very potent brand of sexuality.

She stopped in the hallway when she spied his overnight bag. It looked expensive. As she'd told him, he had a fully stocked wardrobe in his suite, but she should probably take his bag up too. Wasn't that part of the job spec of a housekeeper?

She went back upstairs and halted at his door, suddenly uncertain. It was half closed. She couldn't hear anything, so she knocked lightly and cleared her throat. It felt weird, after having had the house to herself.

There was no response, so she pushed the door open. Then she saw the door leading to the en suite bathroom was half open. There was the sound of running water, and tendrils of steam drifted out. He was in the shower.

Maggie crept forward and put the bag on the bed, turning to make a hasty retreat. Before she did, though, she looked in the direction of the bathroom and saw a tall, dark shape. The water wasn't running any more. And she stood, transfixed, as Nikos Marchetti's body was revealed in the sliver of space at the open doorway as the steam evaporated.

She couldn't move. There was a roaring in her head. He was naked and he was...*magnificent*. Breathtaking. Long, lean limbs. Hard-muscled torso. Every inch of olive skin gleamed and rippled. The hair on his chest led in a line down to the curling hair between his legs where—Maggie's face flamed—she could see the evidence of just how potent his body was.

And then he stilled.

Maggie's gaze moved up and she was caught in the beam of those dark gold and green eyes. Totally unperturbed, Nikos Marchetti reached for a towel and slung it around his narrow hips, covering his body. He didn't say a word.

As if someone had come along and slapped her across the face, to break her out of her stasis, Maggie got out a garbled, 'Sorry… I thought you might need…something…your bag…'

Then she turned and fled from the room, body and face burning.

Nikos drained his glass of the white wine that had accompanied a surprisingly delicious chicken stew. He hadn't realised how hungry he was until Maggie had placed it in front of him in the less formal of the dining rooms and the smell had made his stomach rumble. Food was rarely more than a means to keep going in his world.

He sat back now, ruminating on the fact that everything about this evening had been surprising.

Such as arriving here to find his housekeeper at least twenty years younger than he'd expected. And beautiful. And sexy in a way that caught at Nikos deep inside, where most women didn't impact on him. He liked to keep things superficial. Light. He wasn't in the market for anything deeper after a lifetime's learning that his emotional needs wouldn't ever be met. He focused on transitory pleasures and amassing his fortune—staking his claim on the family business.

Maggie reappeared in the doorway. She'd changed her clothes since that explosive moment when he'd looked up and caught her staring at him as if she'd never seen a naked man before. Like a rabbit caught in the headlights. Her huge blue eyes big and round and fixated on that part of him that had refused to cool down in spite of turning his shower to cold for several long seconds at the end.

It was a good thing she'd left when she had or she'd have seen just how potent her effect on him was. He'd had to get back into the shower and turn it to cold for long minutes, resisting the urge to take the edge off his acute desire. He *wasn't* at the mercy of his body and hormones—no matter how tempting his housekeeper was.

She now wore a white shirt tucked neatly into black trousers. Flat black brogues. Hair pulled back into a bun at the back of her head. And, bizzarely, even though she was conforming exactly to the way he would have expected his housekeeper to behave, it irritated him intensely.

Yet he couldn't fault her. The house was pristine. And he had been out of line arriving without any notice. She worked here—she couldn't be expected to be in a state of readiness twenty-four/seven. That was just…not feasible.

She came over, avoiding his eye, and picked up the plate.

He said, 'That was very good. Excellent, in fact. You said you made it?'

Maggie was doing her best to avoid eye contact with Nikos Marchetti. But she couldn't ignore him. She forced herself to look at him. His hair was still damp and curling thickly on his head. Which only reminded her of *that moment*…

She said quickly, 'I used to work as a commis chef in a restaurant. That's what I want to do eventually…be a chef.'

Nikos Marchetti frowned. 'Why did you leave?'

Maggie wished that the clothes she'd put on—her uniform—felt like a barrier against that dark gaze. But when he looked at her she felt as if he was seeing all the way through her to where her blood was rushing and still felt so hot.

'Because of my mother's illness. Also, the head chef was too handsy for my liking.'

Nikos Marchetti tensed visibly. 'You mean he touched you?'

Maggie was surprised at his reaction. 'Me and pretty much every other female member of staff who came within a few feet of him. But my mother fell ill, so it wasn't a hard decision to come here to help her. She thought she could manage with my help. But then her illness progressed quickly…'

Nikos Marchetti stood up and took the plate out of Maggie's hands. He pulled out a chair. 'Sit down.'

Maggie hesitated for a moment, but then sat down. Nikos Marchetti sat down too.

'I'm sorry about earlier. Someone should have rung ahead to tell you of my arrival. And I'm sorry about your mother. You were lucky to have had her as long as you did. You sound as if you were close.'

Maggie looked at her boss. Maybe if she kept reaffirming that in her head—*her boss*—she would be able to ignore the way there seemed to be a million signals between them going on under the surface. Her awareness of him...the way he looked at her. It was illictly thrilling.

'We *were* close. She was a single parent and I was an only child.'

'Your father wasn't on the scene?'

Maggie shook her head quickly. 'No, he wasn't.' In a bid to divert him away from a subject she avoided like the plague, she asked, 'Is *your* mother still alive?'

Instantly Nikos Marchetti's expression shuttered. 'No. She died a long time ago. I don't remember her at all.'

For some reason Maggie had a sense that wasn't entirely true. But she said, 'I'm sorry. Losing a parent at any age is tough.' She reached out to take his plate again and stood up. 'If you'd like to move into the lounge I can bring you coffee, or tea?'

Nikos Marchetti looked at her and for a moment it was as if he'd forgotten she was there. He'd disappeared for a second.

Maggie suspected that the persona he projected—rich, careless—was a little bit of a construct, hiding something far more formidable under the surface. He was watchful, even though he carried that careless air of nonchalance.

'I'll have a whiskey. But on one condition.'

Maggie had been turning away and now looked back. Nikos Marchetti was standing up. 'What condition?' she asked. For some reason her heart tripped into a faster rhythm.

'That you join me for a glass. It's the least I can do after arriving unannounced.'

Maggie's hands tightened on the plate. She felt breathless again, just imagining inhabiting the same space as this man. Especially after seeing him naked.

'That's really not necessary.'

'Please. I've had more scintillating conversation with you in the last couple of hours than I've had with anyone in the last month. Indulge me.'

CHAPTER TWO

NIKOS WAITED IN the living room for Maggie to return. He didn't know if she'd take him up on his offer and realised it had been a long time since a woman had held any element of surprise for him.

He was used to not having to fight very hard or work very hard to get what he wanted—women or deals. He knew this was largely thanks to his genes and his wealth. He was under no illusions that if those elements were stripped away his life would be very different.

Still, life had become…boring of late.

He stood at the open French doors. The air was warm and still. Nothing was moving. A lone cow mooed in the distance. He couldn't recall the last time he'd been somwhere so peaceful, and to his surprise it wasn't making him itch for distraction—it was soothing his ragged edges.

No one knew he was here. That had been one of the indefinable things that had appealed to him about this house. The fact that it was so rural—a complete contrast to the life he usually led—had

made his spontaneous purchase even more surprising. But he didn't want to analyse that now.
And he certainly didn't want to analyse the sensation that he was in a place that felt like home,
when nowhere had *ever* felt like home to him.

He didn't have a home and he didn't want one.
Home was a myth.

He went over and looked at the bookshelves
that lined one wall. Something caught his attention. He reached out and pulled a book off the
shelf. It had been a childhood favourite of his,
and it immediately and disconcertingly took him
back in time to when he'd used books as a form
of escape in his younger years.

He heard a sound and looked round. Maggie
was coming in with a tray. Immediately he noticed the two glasses beside the bottle of whiskey.
The rush of anticipation that coursed through him
might have surprised him in another setting, but
this evening had thrown up so many surprises
that he barely noticed.

She stopped when she saw the book in his
hand. She looked sheepish. 'Sorry, I put some
of my books on the shelves. I hope you don't
mind...'

Nikos put the book back. 'It's no big deal. I'm
surprised you still have your childhood books.'

Maggie wasn't meeting his eyes now, as she
put the tray down. He was used to women being

forward, taking advantage of his interest. She was different. And he wanted her.

She poured whiskey into both glasses. She handed him one, kept one.

He lifted his. 'Cheers.'

She came closer, tapped her glass on his quickly. 'Cheers.'

She took a sip and made a face as the tart drink burned the back of her throat.

He smiled at her reaction. 'Not a whiskey drinker?'

Maggie shook her head. 'I've always wanted to try it.'

'So that's why you agreed to have a drink with me? In the interest of research?'

'Something like that,' Maggie said, hoping to sound careless, as if this interaction with the most dynamic man she'd ever met wasn't as intimidating as it felt.

She sneaked a glance at him. He was looking right at her. Her gaze skittered away again, but not before she saw what looked like a glint of humour in his eyes. As if he knew exactly what kind of effect he was having on her.

'So tell me—how did your books survive for so long?'

Maggie felt ridiculously nervous. 'We moved around a lot, me and my mother, when I was young. Books were my escape in a world that kept changing. My one constant. I'm kind of superstitious about them now. It's silly...'

'Not silly at all. I get it.'

'You do?' She was surprised. Again.

He grimaced faintly. 'I had those books too. But they got left behind long ago and I never really read much again. Didn't have time.'

Maggie felt a little ache near her heart that she shouldn't be feeling for a near total stranger. 'I wouldn't have had you down as a bookworm,' she remarked.

Nikos arched a brow. 'I'm more than just a pretty face.'

Maggie couldn't stop the smile tugging at her mouth. He'd said that with a definite mocking edge that he didn't need—because it was the truth. He was gorgeous. Overwhelmingly so. And she suspected that he was a *lot* more than just a pretty face. His eyes were way too sharp and knowing. Cynical.

Nikos had opened the French doors and everything was still outside. As if the rest of the world was very far away. But in spite of the stillness and the peace there was an elecricity running through her veins. Dangerous. Thrilling.

He asked, 'You aren't bored here? It seems like an odd job for a beautiful young woman.'

Maggie's heart hitched. *Beautiful?* She told

herself he must say that to dozens of women. An easy platitude. She felt self-conscious. Defensive.

'Since my mother died I've appreciated a…a quiet space to mourn her.' She wrinkled her nose. 'But in any case I'm not really the clubbing type.'

Except right now the thought of clubbing was almost attractive. A way to defuse the intensity of the atmosphere in the room between her and Nikos Marchetti. Which she had to be imagining. A man like him moved in circles far removed from country houses in quiet rural Ireland.

That prompted her to ask, 'Why did you buy this house?'

He arched a brow. 'I need a reason?'

Embarrassed, she said, 'Of course not…it just doesn't seem like the kind of place for a man like…' She trailed off, mortified now.

'It's an investment. I thought I might buy some race horses in the future, and I'd need a house with stables.'

Maggie didn't fully believe this perfectly plausible explanation. And she didn't even know why. She hardly knew this man.

'What prompted you to come here this evening?' she asked.

'Has anyone ever told you you ask a lot of questions?' he said.

Maggie flushed and smiled sheepishly. 'My mother—all the time. Maggie the Inquisitor, she used to call me.'

* * *

Once again Nikos was surprised by how honest she was, and the way she seemed to have no fear of him. It was refreshing. And arousing.

The truth was that he'd come here because he'd wanted to escape the claustrophobic confines of that function. He'd intended flying straight back to London, but the next scheduled flight wasn't until the following morning, and Nikos refused to use private air transport unless absolutely necessary.

He'd been about to book a hotel. But then he'd remembered his house. The house he'd never even visited. And so he'd come here feeling restless. Unsettled.

And then she'd opened the door and his brain had seized in a paroxysm of lust.

As if sensing the direction of his thoughts, she drained her glass and put it down on the tray. 'Thank you for the drink, but if you'll just tell me what time you want breakfast I'll have it ready for you in the morning.'

She looked at him and all he could see were those huge blue eyes. The two pink spots of colour in her cheeks. A pulse beating hectically in her neck. Breasts rising and falling under her shirt with her breaths.

The chemistry between them was so tangible he could taste it. He knew she wanted him as much as he wanted her. If there was anything he was expert in, it was women and desire.

He said, 'I couldn't care less about breakfast. Are you really going to pretend you don't feel it too?'

Maggie's heart stopped. And then started again in an irregular rhythm. Maybe she'd misheard.

'I'm sorry—what did you say?'

He smiled a slow smile and it was pure sin. She could feel heat creeping up over her chest into her cheeks. So much for hoping to create a more professional atmosphere by cutting this late-night drink short.

'You heard me, Maggie.'

Her name from his mouth… It trailed over her skin like raw silk, leaving goosebumps behind.

She swallowed. 'I don't know what you're talking about. If you'll excuse me, I'm going to go to bed now.'

She turned to leave, skin prickling and heart thumping, even as part of her ached to see just where his words might go. No man had ever had this effect on her. She didn't know how to handle it. How to be blasé, nonchalant. A man like Nikos Marchetti would chew her up and spit her out. Of that she had no doubt.

Before she reached the door, though, he said from behind her, 'Aren't you even curious? Do you know how rare it is to feel chemistry this powerful with another person?'

No! Because she'd never experienced anything like it before and it intimidated the hell out of her even as it thrilled her. She was a virgin, and totally out of her depth with a man like this.

Reluctantly she turned around to face him again. 'I think there must have been plenty of women at your event this evening who would have been only too happy to explore your mutual chemistry.'

He made a face. 'I didn't want any of those women. But the moment I saw you I wanted *you*. That hasn't happened to me in a long time.'

A shiver of longing went through Maggie before she could stop it.

Words, she told herself frantically, *These are just words to entice.*

He was playing with her. She was just a passing fancy.

Angry at herself for her out-of-control reaction, she said, 'I suspect that has more to do with your being jaded than with me personally.'

His mouth hitched at one side. 'You're not wrong. I *am* jaded. And cynical.'

Surprise that he was agreeing with her knocked her off-centre. She hadn't expected it of a man like him.

He shook his head. 'It's a long time since anyone surprised me. But you have, Maggie. If anything, you've reminded me that not everyone or everything is cynical.'

He put down his glass and came towards her. Maggie was rooted to the spot.

He stopped a couple of feet away. 'I'm not a man who plays games. I see what I want and go after it. I want you like I haven't wanted anyone in a very long time. You intrigue me. You excite me. But obviously this is not an ideal situation. Whatever happens is outside the bounds of your job. If you want this, it's between two mutually consenting adults and it's your call. Your decision. I'm getting the first flight back to London tomorrow. I don't know when I'll be back again.'

Maggie couldn't remember if she'd ever known anyone to talk so directly. Not even her no-nonsense Scottish mother. But she struggled to do the right thing over the pounding beat of her pulse. 'I don't think it would be a good idea...'

Nikos Marchetti took a step closer. So close that Maggie could see the gold and green flecks in his eyes. His scent tantalised her nostrils, making her want to move closer. She fought the urge.

'You're probably right—and normally I would never sanction mixing business with pleasure—but I find in this instance that I'm willing to take the risk. If you are.'

She swallowed. 'No, I don't think I am.'

There was a long beat and then he said, 'Okay. Your call. Goodnight, Maggie.'

He walked out of the room and Maggie turned to watch him go. He moved with lithe athletic grace. Broad shoulders tapering down to lean hips. Long legs.

When he'd disappeared she let out a shuddery breath. She lifted a hand and touched her mouth, almost expecting it to be swollen, as if he'd kissed her. He hadn't.

But you'd like him to, whispered a wicked voice.

Maggie groaned softly. Never in her wildest dreams had she imagined that this kind of scenario would present itself. She couldn't be more isolated from the world, and yet one of the sexiest, most dynamic men on the planet had more or less literally dropped into her lap.

He wanted her. And she had never felt this kind of physical attraction before. She'd believed it was a myth—a tale spun in the romantic novels her mother had loved. Maggie prided herself on her more practical outlook. She'd accused Nikos Marchetti of being cynical, but she knew she was cynical too. She was a cynical twenty-three-year-old virgin.

Another shiver went through her, but this time it wasn't one of awareness. Or desire. It was one of foreboding. She'd never intended staying here for ever, but three months had slipped by almost without her noticing. If she wasn't careful she would end up like Miss Havisham from *Great Expectations*—except she wouldn't even be lamenting a ruined relationship—because she'd never had one.

Nikos Marchetti is not offering a relationship. He's offering a moment in time, to explore mutual chemistry.

Maggie guessed that for a man like him— suave, experienced—it was second nature to act on impulses like this: seducing women he desired. He didn't seem like a man who denied himself. And was that such a bad thing? It wasn't as if he'd pretended there was anything else going on here.

On autopilot, Maggie went and closed the French doors. She collected the tray with the whiskey and empty glasses and took them down to the kitchen. Everything was silent and quiet. She could almost imagine for a moment that she'd dreamed up the events of the evening since Nikos Marchetti had knocked on the door so imperiously.

But the seismic changes in her body told her it hadn't been a dream. He hadn't even touched her, but she felt as if she'd been plugged into some vital force. She felt alive. Her skin was sensitive… hot. Her heart was still pounding.

Maggie cursed herself. She'd made a decision a long time ago to forge a different path from her mother, who had been dazzled by a powerful man and then cast aside as if she was rubbish. She'd vowed never to let herself be treated like that. If and when *she* had a relationship, it would be with someone who was her equal. Someone who shared her values—who wanted a simple wholesome life. Someone who took responsibility for their actions.

And if and when she had children she would want them to grow up in one place, safe and secure. Not wondering what they'd done to make their father hate them so much that he'd reject them for fear they'd lay claim to his fortune.

She wanted her children to grow up with two parents. She knew how hard it was to do it alone. She'd spent the guts of the last year caring for her rapidly diminishing mother, and some of her mother's last words had been about her regret that she hadn't met someone else, to give Maggie a more stable environment. Maggie had only realised then how lonely her mother must have been.

So the fact that she was even thinking about Nikos Marchetti and his outrageous suggestion was ridiculous. It was something she should be dismissing out of hand. He was the antithesis of everything she'd ever wanted. An arrogant rich man who bought vast houses on a whim and never visited them.

He's not asking for a relationship, reminded that small voice.

Maggie didn't have to be experienced to know

that a man like Nikos Marchetti would not be looking for anything that wasn't transitory.

She felt hopelessly conflicted.

Would it really be so bad to take something for herself? When she'd never behaved selfishly in her life?

Just for a moment in time?

Nikos Marchetti was under this roof for one night. Based on his track record, he wouldn't be back for ages. If ever.

A million butterflies erupted in Maggie's belly and she put a hand there, as if that would quell them.

Maybe if she hadn't actually seen him naked…

But, no… She couldn't possibly be considering—*could* she? *No!*

She shut down her feverish mind and went and briskly turned off the lights, made her way upstairs. Her room was the most modest—tucked in a return, away from the main bedrooms. But she hesitated on the landing.

She could go into her bedroom, shut her door, and Nikos Marchetti would most likely be gone before she even woke in the morning. Temptation gone. The moment passed. Her world would never collide with his again. She moved in circles far outside of his sphere. By the time he returned to the house again she probably would have moved on to another job.

And still be a virgin.

As that stark thought sank in, a kind of reck-lessness she'd never experienced before rose up inside her. Nikos Marchetti was offering some-thing decadent and illicit. He was offering life, and vitality. And, after seeing her mother wither away, Maggie desperately needed to feel that life force.

Almost of their own volition her feet turned in the other direction. She walked down the corridor towards Nikos Marchetti's bedroom. She stopped at the door, feeling slightly light-headed with the enormity of what she was contemplating.

She raised her hand and saw it was shaking. She lowered it again. She couldn't do this. She wasn't experienced enough to take what Nikos Marchetti was offering and remain unscathed. As tempted as she was, he would scorch her alive.

She turned away—and came face to face with fire.

Nikos Marchetti was standing in the corridor, naked from the waist up. Sweat pants hung low from his hips and he had a towel slung around his shoulders. His hair was damp. Face flushed. His dark olive skin gleamed. Dimly, she realised he must have been in the gym.

If Maggie had had a moment to resist then it had passed. He took a step closer and she could smell him. Musky and thrillingly masculine.

'Maggie?'

She dragged her gaze up from where it had

been fixated on the dark curling hair covering his pectorals. 'Yes?'

'I presume you're not here to check if I have everything I need?'

She knew that she could quite easily step around him and continue on back to her bedroom. If she wanted to. Which she didn't.

Slowly, she shook her head.

'Do you know what you're doing?'

No, said an inner voice. But she nodded jerkily. 'I... I think so.'

Nikos Marchetti stepped closer. So close that she could see how his eyes glittered.

'You need to be sure, Maggie. I won't accept anything less.'

A deep, intense longing settled in her core. She couldn't turn her back on this. 'I am sure.'

'Nikos,' he said.

She blinked. 'You want me to say your name?'

He nodded.

Somehow it would have been less daunting if he'd just taken her face in his hands and kissed her.

She opened her mouth, took a breath, her heart thumping unevenly. 'Nikos,' she said.

Another shiver went through her. It felt unbearably intimate. His name on her tongue. He was no longer the owner of this house, and she wasn't his housekeeper. They were equal.

As if reading her mind, he said, 'When we go

through that door we go as two mutually consenting adults, Maggie. You do not have to do anything you don't want. You don't owe me anything because of who I am. You are doing this because you want to. Because we both want this.'

She found that she felt quite touched that he was being so careful to make sure she felt in control of the situation. Again, not something she would have expected of a man like him.

'I know what I'm doing. I want this.' Maggie's voice was husky.

'Good.'

Nikos came forward and took Maggie's hand in his. He led her into the bedroom, where lamps shed pools of golden light around the room. The sky was still a very dark lavender outside. On these summer nights there was only a few hours of total darkness.

He let her hand go and faced her. He made a face. 'I should shower.'

The thought of him turning away from her, even for a small moment, made her feel panicky—as if she might lose her nerve. 'No, you don't need to,' she said.

And he didn't. He smelled divine.

He pulled the towel off his shoulders and threw it down on a nearby chair. Then he said, 'Come here.'

Maggie took the step towards him, her skin

tight all over, prickling with anticipation and awareness.

'Take down your hair.'

She reached behind her, as if in a dream, and pulled her hair loose. It fell around her shoulders. Unruly hair. Thick and unmanageable. Too much. But it was the same as her mother's so she loved it.

So, apparently, did Nikos. He reached out, taking a long strand and twining it around his fingers. 'Your hair is amazing...'

He tugged her even closer. Maggie's legs were like jelly. He slid the hand holding her hair around her neck, his thumb over the pulse that was hammering against her skin.

He tipped her jaw up. 'Touch me.'

Maggie lifted her hands and put them on Nikos's chest, felt his hair scratching her palms, his skin warm and alive. Muscles tensed under her fingers. Suddenly there wasn't enough oxygen in the room, even though Maggie felt a faint breeze coming from an open window.

Nikos put his other hand on Maggie's arm and bent his head, his breath feathering over her mouth for a moment. She smelled whiskey, and it rushed to her head all over again.

Everything inside her went still as she waited for his mouth to touch hers. She felt superstitiously that nothing would be the same after this... And then his mouth settled over hers and she knew it wasn't a superstition. It was truth.

Like dry kindling to a match, she went up in flames.

Nothing could have prepared her for how Nikos's mouth felt on hers—how it moved and enticed, encouraging her to open up so he could explore the very depths of her.

And the deeper the kiss got, the hungrier she became. It was as if she'd been starved her whole life until this moment. His hand was in her hair again now, tugging her head back to allow him more access, and Maggie moved closer, seeking more contact. She was responding instinctively, from a primal place of need...

Nikos was drowning in heat and lust. Maggie's mouth under his...hesitant and soft at first, and then becoming bolder...ignited his senses like no other woman ever had, blasting apart any jadedness or ennui.

Her body was quivering against his like a taut bow. Full breasts were pressed against his chest, and he itched to explore her curves, explore every womanly inch of her. Her height was a novelty he relished.

He found the front of her shirt, his hands uncharacteristically inexpert, and undid the buttons, pushing the shirt apart. He pulled back from her mouth and opened his eyes, groaned softly. Her eyes were still closed, lashes long and dark on her cheeks, and her mouth was plump and pink.

She opened her eyes and it took a second for them to focus on him.

Desire wound tight as a drum inside Nikos. When was the last time he'd kissed such a responsive woman? Perhaps when he'd been a teenager, fumbling and awkward?

He looked down and stopped breathing. Her breasts were full and high. Encased in lace. Her waist was small and her hips flared—she embodied a feminine sensuality that he suspected she wasn't even aware of.

She ducked her head but he tipped her chin up. 'You are *stunning*.'

Her cheeks were hot. 'I'm not wearing anything…special.'

Nikos had to control his urge to strip her bare and bury himself to the hilt, seeking immediate relief.

'Believe me, you are the sexiest woman I've ever seen,' he said.

She looked serious. 'You don't have to say things like that.'

'I'm not just saying it…' He meant it. The women he took to bed were usually so confident they required little or no compliments. Maggie seemed…*shy*.

Something occurred to him then and he went still. But he dismissed it out of hand. She might seem inexperienced, but she was probably putting it on—because in this day and age no one her age could be that innocent. She just wasn't worldly or sophisticated…

Maggie looked up at Nikos. For a second she wondered if he suspected how inexperienced she was, and she knew if she was going to say anything then this was her moment. She should tell him.

But all she could see in her mind's eye was the way he would look at her—with shock and then disgust. She felt panicky at the thought of him rejecting her. Surely he wouldn't notice?

A sense of desperation made her say, 'Nikos… I do want this… I want you.'

His eyes grew darker. He pushed the shirt off her shoulders, down her arms, and it fell to the floor. Maggie kicked off her shoes, undid the button on her trousers and pushed them down, stepping out of them.

Now she wore only her underwear, and Nikos's gaze travelled down over her body in a slow and thorough appraisal. Her hands itched and she clenched them into fists. She'd never felt so needy in her life.

With a brisk economy of movement Nikos shed the rest of his clothes until he was naked.

Maggie looked down and gulped. He was hard. Thick and long.

'Touch me, Maggie.'

She wanted to. But suddenly she was shy.

She reached out and traced a finger down his length, over a throbbing vein. She heard a low moan. Was it her or him? She couldn't think straight. She wanted to wrap her hand around him.

But he took her wrist and said, in a choked-sounding voice, 'I'm feeling a little underdressed here…'

Maggie looked up at him. He put his hands on her shoulders and turned her around, undoing her bra and letting it fall forward and off. He tugged her panties over her hips and down. They fell to her feet.

Her breathing was so shallow now she felt dizzy. No one had ever seen her as naked as this. She'd even been shy in front of her mother.

'Turn around, Maggie.'

Slowly she turned around, eyes down. She heard Nikos's indrawn breath. She bit her lip… saw his hand come into her line of vision. He cupped a breast, feeling its weight. His thumb traced the areola around her nipple and it stood to attention. Tight and hard.

Maggie bit her lip so hard she could taste blood. It was excruciatingly intense, the sensation rushing through her body. She'd never expected it could be like this—slow, exploratory… Torturous in the most pleasurable way.

She looked up at Nikos. His eyes were heavy-lidded. Cheeks flushed.

She tried to articulate what she was feeling, 'I can't… I need…'

He looked at her, his hand closing over her plump flesh, trapping her nipple between two fingers. Maggie reached out, her hands landing on his biceps. She had to hold on to something. She was drowning.

'I need…you. More…'

Nikos took his hand from her breast and Maggie almost cried out. He led her over to the wide bed. The bed that she remade every week with fresh linen.

No, don't think about that now.

He came down on the bed beside her, and the clamour of needy voices in her head stopped when he covered her mouth with his again. He explored her with his hands, finding curves she hadn't even been aware of. His mouth moved down, leaving a trail of fire in its wake as he came closer and closer to where she ached most for him to explore: the throbbing points of her breasts.

When his mouth closed over one, encasing it in hot, sucking heat, she arched her back helplessly. Her hands were buried in his hair as he moved from one to the other, his hands plumping her breasts even more, feeding her to himself like some decadent pasha lingering over a tasty meal.

When he moved downwards Maggie was panting. He settled his body between her legs, opening her up to him. She'd never been more exposed, or so much at someone else's mercy, and yet she felt no sense of vulnerability or insecurity. Only a sense of wonder and awe.

He looked up at her and she could only describe the expression on his face as *wicked*—just before he dipped his head and she felt his mouth on her—*right there*—at the most intimate part of her body.

Maggie's hands, no longer in Nikos's hair, found the sheets and gripped them as he mercilessly demonstrated his skill. At one point the feeling was so intense she tried to close her thighs, but he kept them open. He put a hand on her belly, as if to soothe her, while his tongue explored her with a thoroughness that left her dizzy.

Everything inside her was winding tighter and tighter, bringing her to an edge she'd only ever explored on her own before. And then, with a rush, she tipped over the edge, her whole body spasming as a huge wave of pleasure undulated out from the centre of her being. She hadn't expected it to be so violent—like a force rushing through her body that she couldn't hope to contain. A force outside her control.

She looked up, dazed, as Nikos loomed over her. She'd heard the sound of foil ripping and looked down now, to see that he'd sheathed himself with protection. Her muscles quivered with renewed desire. *Already.* What was happening to her? She was insatiable.

Nikos looked at her. 'You're unbelievably responsive...do you know what a turn-on that is?'

Maggie couldn't speak. She could only shake her head.

Nikos moved between her legs and his thighs pushed hers apart a little more. She instinctively shifted, welcoming him into the cradle of her body, still sensitive after the rush of pleasure but already aching for more.

Nikos looked down at her, and then he slid an arm around her back, arching her up to him while at the same time guiding himself into her body, pushing deep in one cataclysmic thrust.

Maggie gasped, clutching at his arms, eyes wide as she absorbed the sensation of his body joining with hers.

Nikos went still, eyes narrowing on her face.

'Maggie...are you—?'

Reacting on pure instinct, and a desperate need for him not to say it out loud, she wrapped her legs around his hips, which deepened his thrust inside her. 'Please, don't stop...'

The sting of pain was fading as Nikos's body pulsed inside hers. She could have cried with relief when he started to move out and then moved back in. She welcomed him, her body flowing and adapting around his as an instinctive rhythm caught their bodies up in its timeless dance.

Nikos held her thigh against him as his thrusts became harder, deeper, faster. And Maggie could only cling on as the storm leapt and danced within her, whirling her higher and higher into a vortex of gathering pleasure that she couldn't escape. Didn't want to escape.

Her body arched up into Nikos's as tension held her taut for a long moment, the pinnacle beckoning, making her desperate for release. And then it broke, hurling her high over and over again, not letting her catch her breath as her whole being pulsated and throbbed in the aftermath.

Nikos knew she wasn't even aware of him tensing over her body as he, too, found his release, his body spasming deep inside her in the strongest climax he'd ever experienced, turning him inside out.

It tore through his body so powerfully that for a moment he could ignore the truth that had seared itself onto his brain before she'd pushed him over the edge and to the point of no return.

She'd been a virgin.

CHAPTER THREE

MAGGIE LAY ON the bed, unable to move. The aftershocks of what had just happened still rippled through her, inside, where Nikos's body had filled her to the point of almost pain…and then such pleasure as she'd never known could exist.

He'd gone into the bathroom, and Maggie was glad of a moment's respite to try and absorb what had happened. How it had made her feel. She hadn't expected it to be so…so intensely exquisite. So bone-shakingly desperate.

She heard the bathroom door open and pulled the sheet over herself. Nikos emerged with a towel slung around his waist. The sheer magnificence of his body made her mouth go dry. To think that a man like him had wanted her…

And then he spoke.

'Why didn't you tell me you were a virgin?'

He'd noticed.

Maggie's insides dropped like a stone. Of course he'd noticed.

She looked at him and couldn't speak. Not

yet. Still too shocked at what had happened. The speed at which she'd gone from dealing with the unexpected arrival of her absentee boss to this moment was truly mortifying. As was her total and absolute capitulation. He hadn't even had to touch her to seduce her!

Now he looked the opposite of seductive. He looked positively icy. Condemning. A cold shiver went down her spine. *What had she done?*

She made her mouth form the shape of a word. 'I...'

'You...?' he said, impatience and something else less definable making his tone sharp.

Maggie's brain wouldn't function. She dragged her gaze away from his naked torso. 'Can you put some clothes on, please?'

He emitted a curse in some language that sounded guttural. She took advantage of the fact that he'd moved towards where his trousers lay, in a crumpled heap on the floor to pull the sheet up over her breasts.

He came back, hitching his trousers over his hips, pulling up the zip. 'Well?'

Maggie wanted to point out that his top button was still open but she resisted the urge. She swallowed. Focused on his question.

Virgin.

'I didn't think...' She trailed off.

That had been the problem, from the moment he'd appeared on the doorstep earlier she hadn't had a rational thought in her head. First of all she'd sparked off him, and then...then she'd wanted him.

He opened his mouth, but she didn't want to hear that sharp tone again so she said, with a little sheepishness, 'I didn't want you to stop.'

I was afraid you'd stop. Those words trembled on her lips but she clamped her mouth shut.

'*Theos,* Maggie. You should have told me. I thought you were experienced. I don't sleep with virgins. I am the last man who should initiate a woman in her first sexual experience.'

Maggie's body disagreed. After what had just happened, the thought of another man being the one to initiate her in the ways of lovemaking almost made her feel nauseous.

And that was an earth-shattering revelation.

Wasn't Nikos Marchetti the antithesis of everything she wanted in a man?

At what point had she succumbed to his wicked temptation?

It was all fuzzy now, but Maggie knew that somewhere along the way she'd justified having sex with him. And now she felt exposed. She'd had sex with a man who was the same as her father: rich and powerful. And she'd done it without a second thought.

She said, 'Could you pass me a robe, please?'

Nikos looked at Maggie for a long moment, feeling conflicted between anger and desire. She looked thoroughly and utterly debauched. Her skin was still pink from his touch. Her hair was in a wild tumble around her shoulders. Her lips were swollen. Her eyes were huge with the same conflict he was feeling, but there was also something slumberous. And dazed. As if she couldn't believe what had just happened.

Neither could he. He hadn't had such an erotic encounter in a long time. If ever. He'd never felt such desperation to join his body to a woman's.

He emitted a frustrated sound and retrieved a robe from the bathroom door, handing it to Maggie, who scooted into it awkwardly, trying not to show her skin.

It didn't really work. Nikos still got a view of one plump breast and recalled how his hand hadn't been able to contain its bounty.

His body tightened again. He ran a hand through his hair.

Maggie belted the robe and stood up from the bed. It was no consolation to see her legs wobble slightly. His own didn't feel much steadier.

Nikos shook his head. 'How were you still innocent?'

She shrugged minutely, avoiding his eye. 'I just…never met anyone I wanted to…' A blush stained her cheeks red.

'Have sex with?' he supplied, with a tone that he knew was astringent.

She looked at him. 'Something like that.'

There was something defiant in her eyes now. Proud. It impacted on Nikos down low in his gut, pulling everything tight again. Making him want *more*.

Then she said, 'That was a mistake.'

The strength of the rejection he felt at hearing her say that surprised him. He shook his head. 'Oh, no, *angeli mou*—it's a bit late for regrets. We knew what we were doing—or are you now going to claim that you didn't?'

His conscience struck him. She'd been innocent, so technically she hadn't really known.

Anger eclipsed his conscience. He said again, 'You should have told me you were a virgin.'

She looked at him. 'You're right. I should have, maybe then we would have come to our senses.'

The thought of the dilemma Nikos would have faced had he known of Maggie's innocence wasn't lost on him. Would he have had the strength to deny himself? In spite of his lofty assertion that he didn't sleep with virgins?

And his pride was piqued. 'Do you really mean that?'

She flushed pinker. 'I'm disappointed in myself for sleeping with someone like you.'

Shock and indignation rocked through Nikos. No woman—*ever*—voiced regret for sleeping with him. The opposite, in fact.

He folded his arms. 'Someone like me? Please elaborate.'

* * *

Maggie regretted saying anything, but she couldn't escape or prevaricate. Nikos's laser-like gaze wouldn't allow it.

'Someone rich and entitled. Privileged.'

Her conscience pricked. She knew her judgement of him wasn't entirely rational, but from the moment she'd seen him he'd got under her skin and impacted on her in a place where no one ever had before.

After the lessons learnt in her own life, and from her mother, she'd hoped she'd be immune to the lure of a man like him. Cynical. Street-smart. But apparently not.

'Being rich and privileged isn't always all it's cracked up to be—or haven't you read the books and watched the movies about poor little rich kids?'

Maggie's skin prickled uncomfortably. There was a mocking tone to his voice, but also something almost bleak.

She said, 'You're right—that's not fair. It's just...you turned up here, on your first visit to a house you bought sight unseen—'

'Which is really none of your business.'

Maggie clamped her mouth shut, afraid of what might come out next.

Nikos moved closer. The chilly atmosphere warmed slightly.

'The truth is that even if you'd told me you were

innocent I'm not sure if I could have resisted the temptation. Are you really saying you're stronger than that? That if you'd had a moment to think about it you would have changed your mind?'

Maggie couldn't look away from those leonine eyes. Who was she kidding? She *had* had a moment to think about it and she'd chosen *him*.

She shook her head jerkily.

'Neither of us were prepared for this chemistry,' he said. 'What happened was mutual, and I for one do not regret one moment. Regrets are for losers. Own what you want, Maggie. You can't go back—only forward.'

'Forward...' she repeated.

He nodded, and as he did so he reached for her, putting his hands on her robe, tugging her towards him. Treacherously, she didn't resist. So much for her brave declaration.

'What I propose is that we live for the moment and enjoy this very potent mutual desire. Or do you want your initiation to end here?'

Maggie's insides tightened and her skin prickled. Heat licked at her core, making her feel needy and greedy again. Would it be so bad to indulge? One more time? *Did* she want her initiation to end here? Even if it was with the kind of man she'd always sworn she would steer well clear of?

She gave him the only answer she could. 'No...'

Nikos's hands went to Maggie's belt and he slowly undid it, looking at her as if to make sure she really wanted this. Now that she was being honest with herself she felt almost impatient. She wanted to seize every moment of this…whatever it was. One-night stand. Interlude.

Nikos pulled the robe apart and looked at her. The heat at her core spread outwards and en-flamed every nerve-ending and cell. She reached for Nikos's trousers, pulling down the zip. She tugged them down, over his hips and they fell to the floor, revealing his naked potency.

He pushed the robe from her body. They were both naked, and in that moment Maggie felt something emotional wash through her. No mat-ter how conflicted he made her feel, she wouldn't have wanted to share this deepest intimacy with anyone else. She was glad it was him. He was a man she barely knew, and yet she felt she knew him in a way she couldn't really understand.

He pulled her down onto the bed and they landed in a tangle of limbs, hard against soft. Her breasts were pressed against his hard chest.

He put a hand in her hair and tugged her head back. He smiled wickedly and said, 'Don't give yourself a hard time, Maggie. I'm quite irresistible.'

She might have huffed at that assertion—but then his mouth was on hers, and his other hand was on her breast, and she could only agree.

Hours later, when dawn was breaking outside, Maggie lay in a half-slumber, sated beyond anything she'd ever felt before. Her bones felt as if they had liquefied. Nikos's heart beat a steady strong rhythm under her cheek, where she rested on his chest.

That emotion she'd felt earlier was still there, and she knew how dangerous it was to be feeling anything for this man. But she couldn't help wondering about him. Where would he go from here? What was his life like?

A thought chilled her—he could have a mistress, a girlfriend? Although *girlfriend* sounded far too pedestrian for a man like Nikos Marchetti.

As if he could hear her thoughts, he lifted her hand and brought it to his mouth, pressing a kiss to the palm. Which did not help her rogue emotions.

'Okay?' he asked.

Maggie's heart thumped. He was just being solicitous. Again, not something she would have expected.

She lifted her head and looked at him, nodded.

He flipped them so that Maggie was under him. He twined her fingers with his and held her hand above her head.

She couldn't help blurting out, 'Are you seeing anyone at the moment? I mean, is there a girl—*woman*—somewhere? Because I wouldn't like to think that we...' She trailed off, feeling self-conscious.

Nikos went still. 'No. I'm not. I can be accused

of many things, Maggie, but I don't sleep around on women.' Then he frowned as he looked down at her. 'But you need to know this doesn't go beyond this room…tonight. Now. I don't do relationships, Maggie. I'm not interested in settling down, or romance, or happy-ever-afters. They don't exist—or they certainly don't exist with me.'

His words sank into her like cold little stones. She longed to ask him why, but she caught herself. He was telling her what she needed to hear—Nikos Marchetti wasn't the type of man she should want anything more with. Not in a million years.

And yet she'd been drawn to him like a moth to a flame. What did that say about her and her standards? That she was as susceptible as the next woman to his particular potent brand of masculinity?

That she was like her mother, dazzled by the charisma of a powerful man.

A need to protect herself from that too incisive gaze made her say, as lightly as she could, 'Don't worry, I'm under no illusions as to what this is. Anyway, you're not the kind of guy I see myself with long term.'

Nikos was surprised as a little dart of something pierced him. It couldn't possibly be *hurt*.

He moved over her, using his body to push her

thighs apart. He heard her indrawn breath, felt the way she arched against him.

'I'm not?' he asked.

She shook her head, her eyes turning a darker blue. 'No way.'

He nudged her thighs further apart and notched the head of his erection against where she was hot and wet. He knew he had to slow the tempo or he would lose it even before he entered her.

'So...who is this paragon who will serve you for the long term?'

She moved under him restlessly, but that dart of emotion he hadn't welcomed made him torture her a little.

She said breathlessly, 'I don't know...someone kind. Respectful. Considerate. Dependable.'

Nikos made a face. 'Sounds boring.'

Maggie reached up with her free hand and traced the muscles in Nikos's chest. 'Boring is good for long-term happiness.'

Nikos caught her thigh and hitched it up, bringing Maggie's body into closer contact with his. He looked down at her and forced himself to hold back, even though he could feel the sweat breaking out on his brow.

'Just so we know where we stand... Later you can have as boring as you like, but right now... in the short term...you have *me*.'

He surged deep inside her and Maggie's whole

body arched up to his, heightening the mind-melting sensation of joining their bodies.

Nikos let the physical momentum clear his mind of the fact that his encounter with this woman was way out of his usual comfort zone. And every coherent thought dissolved as they raced once again to the shattering peak of pleasure.

Nikos stood looking down at the sleeping Maggie for a long moment. Not the kind of behaviour he usually indulged in. A prickle of unease lay under his skin. He was reluctant to leave. When he *never* stayed. He always moved on.

He didn't like this. *At all.* He felt out of control. At the mercy of a force outside of himself. Exposed.

He blamed the uncharacteristic sense of restlessness that had been plaguing him recently.

He reminded himself that, as erotic as this encounter had been, and as surprising as Maggie had been, she wasn't any different from other women. *She'd just been a virgin.* That was it. That had to be the element that had elevated this experience above all others, distracting him when he knew he should have left already.

She was just a woman, and she'd piqued his interest briefly. Within a few days he'd have moved on and she would have become a dim memory.

The sense he'd had here of coming home was

an illusion, and she'd been part of that illusion. A moment of craziness. But just a moment. Which would not be repeated.

Nikos injected ice into his veins and turned and walked out, already thinking ahead to the things he *should* be thinking of, and not lingering on a virgin Viking Queen who had given up her innocence with such artless passion.

When Maggie woke up the sun was streaming into the bedroom. She was disorientated—and then it all came back. She was in the master suite. Because she'd slept with the master.

She looked around. No sign of Nikos Marchetti. Everything felt very silent and still. The sheet was over her breasts, as if someone had pulled it up.

She came up on one elbow, her hair falling over one shoulder. She felt hollowed out from an overload of sensation, her body aching in places she hadn't known she had muscles.

She saw the robe at the end of the bed and reached for it, pulling it on and getting out of the bed. She noticed that Nikos's clothes weren't scattered on the floor as they had been before.

The nape of her neck prickled.

The bathroom was empty.

She went out of the bedroom and down the corridor. She checked the kitchen. But even before she checked the study and the main living room she knew that she was alone.

He'd gone. Left.

Maggie went into the hall, and it was there that she saw the card propped up on the table, addressed to her with a slashing line in dark ink: *Maggie*.

She opened it.

Thank you for last night, I enjoyed it.
I apologise for the lack of notice. It won't happen again.
Remember, no regrets.
If you need anything, contact my team.
Nikos

It took a long moment for the full impact of the note to hit her. It was like a slow punch to her belly, spreading outwards and making her feel cold. He hadn't even left her his personal number.

Contact my team.

He couldn't have made it any clearer that what had happened had been a very transitory moment.

But isn't that what you signed up to? asked a small voice.

Maggie put the note down. Yes, it was exactly what she'd signed up to—so she shouldn't be feeling this…this wrench.

She just hadn't expected him to be so tender.

Generous. Passionate. She hadn't expected sex to be such a transformative, transcendental experience. She hadn't expected to...to *like* him. She hadn't expected to want to know more about him. To sense that his very charming exterior hid a far more steely interior.

Maggie's history had taught her to be wary, but Nikos had turned her preconceptions and her fears on their head.

Before she knew what she was doing she found herself in the study, turning on the main computer.

She put Nikos's name into the computer search engine. Hundreds of hits came up straight away. Business deals... A new casino recently acquired in Monte Carlo... Lurid headlines alluding to his playboy reputation.

There were other headlines too: speculation about him and his two half-brothers, about who really held the reins of power in the family business.

She barely glanced over the few pictures of him with his half-brothers, who looked equally physically impressive. Her eye was drawn treacherously to the pictures of him with dozens of different women on his arm at various events. They were all beautiful—stunning—and well out of Maggie's league. Not one woman appeared twice.

She felt a little nauseous now when she thought of how easily he'd seduced her. Had he just been intrigued because she wasn't as polished as the women he usually hung out with?

Clearly he was a renowned playboy—as if she hadn't deduced that for herself when he'd left her the way he had. When he'd seduced her with such ease. The fact that he was *known* for this kind of behaviour only took the sting away slightly.

But she shouldn't be feeling any sting. No doubt she was already just a blip in his memory as he flew high over the Irish Sea back to his jet-set lifestyle. A lifestyle that didn't impress her or tempt her in any way.

If anything, she should be feeling lighter. She'd lost her virginity to a consummate master of the arts. The problem was she had a sick feeling that he'd ruined her for any other man.

Nikos's words came back. *'I don't do relationships... I'm not interested in happy-ever-afters.'*

She welcomed the reminder—because the last thing Maggie Taggart wanted was for history to repeat itself and for her to fall in love with a rich and powerful man. Or, worse, have his baby. Nikos Marchetti was a man in her father's mould—avowedly anti-relationship and anti-family. The kind of man Maggie had promised herself she wouldn't ever seek out.

So, if anything, she should be grateful that Nikos Marchetti had spelled it out so brutally—because he was the last man she would ever consider as a long-term partner or as a father for her children.

Literally the last man.

CHAPTER FOUR

A year later

THE CHAUFFEUR-DRIVEN CAR wound its way through the small country roads, tall hedges on either side. The sky was turning a dusky lavender as the sun set and the smell from the farming fields around them was pungent.

The sense of déjà-vu was strong. As was the sense of anticipation that Nikos could not push down.

But she wasn't there.

She'd given in her notice about two weeks after that night they'd spent together. Him and the Viking Queen…

In spite of his best efforts to forget her she'd haunted him all year. His memory of that night was so vivid and potent that she'd ruined him for any other woman. His shock and surprise that any lover could linger so effectively in his memory had turned to serious frustration—so much so that he'd even looked for her.

To no avail. She'd disappeared and she hadn't given his staff any contact details or a forwarding address.

This was unprecedented for Nikos. The fact that he could still want a woman after one night and that she wasn't pursuing him. He wasn't so arrogant to think he was irresistible, but his wealth and fame made him a seductive package to most women.

But she'd been different. A virgin. Sparky. Not intimidated. Passionate. Responsive. Theos. So responsive.

In the back of the car Nikos's body hardened at the memory. He cursed again, then said to the driver curtly, 'How much further?'

The driver's eyes met his in the mirror, 'Almost there, Mr Marchetti.'

Nikos sat back, feeling on edge. His fingertips drummed impatiently on his thigh—a habit he hated and strived to hide around anyone but himself, fearing it showed some kind of weakness.

He was only here because he'd accepted an invitation to his friend's end-of-summer party at a house nearby. It was the same friend who had encouraged him to buy Kildare House and invest in horse racing. An investment he'd never followed up.

As the car finally swept in through the gates of the house Nikos vowed to put the property up for sale as soon as he returned to Paris. It was ridiculous to keep it now. Ridiculous to have kept it for so long.

They pulled up at the bottom of the steps leading to the main door. Nikos took his compact weekend bag out of the boot before the driver could do it.

He knocked on the door, and in the few seconds before it opened he found himself holding his breath, wondering if just maybe…

The door opened. His sense of disappointment was a further mockery to his already jagged edges. This housekeeper couldn't have been more different from Maggie Taggart. For a start he was a man. And somewhere in his fifties.

'Mr Marchetti, how nice to welcome you to Kildare House.'

Nikos stepped inside, aware of how this welcome was so very different from last year's, when he'd had to prove his identity. 'Thank you—Mr Wilson, isn't it?'

'Yes. Here, let me take your bag. I've prepared some coffee and snacks—they're in the living room. I can show you the way—'

Nikos was already striding out of the reception hall, 'I know where it is.'

He went inside and moved straight to the bookshelves. Maggie's books were gone. For a moment something prickled at the back of Nikos's neck. Had he dreamed it all? Dreamed her? Was he so jaded and burnt out from years of carousing and living down to the scandalous reputation he'd so painstakingly built that he'd conjured up a virgin to—

'Will there be anything else, sir?'

Nikos turned around. Mr Wilson stood in the doorway. Not Maggie. The disappointment was as unwelcome as it was acute.

'Just my tuxedo for this evening, please—and let the driver know we'll be leaving in an hour.'

'Of course.'

Nikos looked at the coffee on the tray on the table and made a face. He needed something stronger than coffee to burn away those memories. And what he needed was the taste of another woman to wash the memory of Maggie from his mind and body once and for all. Tonight at the Barbier party there was bound to be at least one woman who would stir Nikos's libido back to life.

Maggie's arms were aching, but she kept a smile fixed to her face as she walked through the crowd, holding the tray full of canapés that she'd helped to make earlier in the Barbier kitchen. Part of the reason she was serving was to gauge the reaction to the canapés.

The scene was magical—an end-of-summer garden party to celebrate the latest successes of the Barbier racing stables and stud. The garden was thronged with men in tuxedoes and women in glittering evening gowns, artfully lit by thousands of candles and fairy lights attached to an elaborate system of webbing that stretched over the garden from tree to tree, creating an intricate canopy of light above their heads.

Maggie saw the hosts in the distance—Luc Barbier and his wife Nessa, who had been a champion jockey until she'd had children. A rush of emotion caught Maggie unawares. They had been so good to her, offering her a job, and then, when she'd—

Her thoughts scattered as she saw a new guest arrive, walking down the steps to be greeted by Luc and Nessa. He was tall and dark. Almost as tall and dark as Luc. Familiar. Ice prickled over her skin.

It couldn't be.

She stopped walking so suddenly that another waiter almost crashed into her.

'Maggie, watch it, will you?'

She didn't even notice someone helping themselves to a canapé. She had to be imagining it—*him*. Her all too frequent dreams had turned into a hallucination. She blinked. Opened her eyes. He was still there, head thrown back now as he laughed at something Luc Barbier was saying.

Women were turning and looking. Whispering. Openly admiring. Lustful. And no wonder. The two men were tall, dark and easily the most gorgeous men in the vicinity—but all Maggie could see was one man. Nikos Marchetti. And all she could remember were those cataclysmic hours when he had transformed her from inexperienced naive virgin into a woman. More than a woman.

Her hands tightened on the tray so much that it shook.

There was a voice near her ear, soft and concerned. 'Maggie? Are you okay? Here, let me take that for you.'

The tray was taken from her hands and Maggie tore her gaze from the man who had moved closer and was now just a few feet away. Nessa Barbier was putting the tray down on a nearby table. Maggie hadn't even noticed her approach.

Nessa's hand was on her arm. 'You look like you've seen a ghost—are you okay?'

Maggie tried to speak, but nothing would come out. This was too huge. Too potentially devastating.

Nessa frowned. 'Maggie, what is it?'

'I… I have to go inside. I need to…' She was babbling, making no sense.

But before she could leave, eyeing up her escape route by skirting around the edge of the crowd, an incredulous voice called her name.

'Maggie?'

Dread pooled in her belly—along with a very belated spark of emotion. *Anger.* She turned around and came face to face with the man she'd tried her best to forget—because he sure as hell hadn't been interested in remembering *her*.

She should have known what to expect. She of all people. But she forced a smile. 'Mr Marchetti. Fancy seeing you here.'

She barely noticed that he looked as shocked, as she felt.

'What are you doing here?'

'I work here.'

'You two know each other?' Nessa sounded intrigued. 'I thought you said he'd never been to Kildare House?'

Maggie winced inwardly. She hadn't actually said that, but she'd been deliberately vague about Nikos's visit last year.

Nikos said, 'I visited the house last year... briefly.'

Yet he'd left a lasting impression—very lasting.

Maggie went cold again as the full significance of Nikos's presence sank in.

Nessa was saying, 'I can't believe you didn't tell us, Nikos...'

Maggie backed away, needing to escape. 'If you'll excuse me...?'

She turned and almost ran towards the house, not even caring what Nessa must be thinking. Because that wasn't important. What was important—

Maggie's hand was caught by another, much bigger hand. 'Hey, wait a second.'

She stopped, felt her heart palpitating. For a big man he moved quickly and quietly.

She pulled her hand free and looked up. She'd forgotten how tall Nikos was. Tall enough to tower over her own not inconsiderable height.

They were near the kitchen entrance of the house and it was dark in this part of the garden. The staff were using another entrance to ferry drinks and canapés from house to garden. Maggie cursed herself for leading him here. It was too quiet…intimate.

Nikos was shaking his head. 'I can't believe you're here.'

Maggie's insides were somersaulting all over the place. Had he always been so broad? Why was she still so aware of him? She needed to remember—not let him distract her.

'Well, I *am* here. Was there something you wanted, Mr Marchetti?'

Electricity crackled between them. The air seemed to grow even heavier, as if there was no oxygen.

His mouth tightened. '*Mr Marchetti?* Really? After—'

'Look,' Maggie cut in, desperate not to have him say it out loud. 'I'm working. I really should get back and—'

'Do you really think they'll miss one waitress for a few minutes? Why did you hand in your notice? Was it because of what happened?'

Maggie swallowed. After two weeks of mooning around the house like a lovestruck calf, in spite of her best intentions, she'd realised that Nikos Marchetti had really meant what he'd said. *Contact my team.*

She'd had a sudden vision of him arriving back at the house at some point in the future with a woman and she'd felt sick. So she'd handed in her notice that day.

She tipped up her chin. 'I was never meant to be your housekeeper. I just took over after my mother died—it was never going to be a long-term thing. It's not as if I had ambitions to be a rich man's housekeeper.'

Nikos's eyes flashed at that. Maggie could see the glint of green and gold in the dim light and it sent fires racing all over her skin.

'So moving down the road to serve finger food at the Barbiers' summer party is a step up?'

Anger sizzled in Maggie's belly and she welcomed it as an antidote to the awful crazy urge she had to plaster herself against this man and beg him to kiss her.

'I'm doing a lot more than just serving canapés. I'm actually making them.'

Nikos took a step closer.

Maggie refused to move back.

'You could have stayed at Kildare House. You didn't have to leave.'

Maggie shook her head. 'No, staying was never an option.'

Why was she suddenly breathless? As if she'd been running.

He tipped his head slightly to one side. 'Actually maybe it *is* better that you left.'

Maggie's brain wouldn't function properly. She couldn't take her eyes off Nikos's firmly sculpted mouth. 'Why?

'Because now there are no issues around me being your boss.'

She dragged her gaze up. 'Why would there be issues?'

'For when we do this...'

He was so close now she could see those hazel glints in his eyes, slightly more gold than green. His hair was a little shorter than last year. There was a day's worth of stubble on his jaw. She had an urge to reach up and feel the prickle against her palm. She curled her hand into a fist.

He reached out and caught a lock of her hair which had escaped the rough bun she'd put it into earlier. She hadn't had her hair cut in...months. It was seriously untamed. Unstyled.

He said, almost to himself, 'I can't believe you're here, right in front of me. You've been a thorn in my side for a year, Maggie Taggart.'

She shook her head, feeling as if she was in a dream. This couldn't be real.

'How...? Why?'

He put his hands on her arms and tugged her towards him gently. 'You've haunted me, mind

and body, and I can't exorcise you until I have you again.'

'Have…have me?' She was stuttering now, the meaning of what he was saying too huge to compute.

He nodded. 'Not one other woman has made me want her the way you did from the moment I saw you. The way you still do. We have unfinished business…'

Maggie was stunned into silence. This was the man who had left her sleeping in his bed a year ago with only a note telling her she should have '*no regrets*' and to contact him through his team if she needed anything.

A million things bombarded her—chiefly indignation. But as his scent wrapped around her she was hurtled back in time and there was a beat thrumming through her blood, drowning out those concerns.

Nikos's head came closer, and then his mouth was covering hers, and as the reality of him flooded her senses Maggie couldn't deny that he'd haunted her too—even though she'd die before admitting it.

His mouth moved over hers as expertly as she remembered, all-consuming. Heat and madness entered her head and body. *Need.* His tongue swept in and sought hers, demanding a response that came willingly, rushing up through her body before she could stop it.

Her hands clutched at his jacket, either to pull him closer or steady her legs—she wasn't sure which. All she knew was that she never wanted the kiss to end. The hunger she felt was greedy, desperate.

But a sense of anger added an edge to her desire. The anger that had been bubbling under the surface at the way he'd left her a year ago, because it had hurt her when it shouldn't have.

Their bodies cleaved together—when had they even moved that close?—chest to chest, hip to hip, thigh to thigh. She felt unbearably soft—liquid next to his steely strength. She was reminded of how small and delicate he made her feel.

He surrounded her, and when he shifted his hips subtly, so she could feel the press of his arousal against her, her lower body clenched in reaction and a spasm of pleasure caught her off guard. It was as if she'd been primed for the last year for exactly this moment, and now it was here and she was ravenous.

How had she survived without this?

What had she been doing?

Nikos's hand was moving from her hip, caressing her waist, then cupping the solid weight of her breast in his hand. Maggie moaned into his mouth as he squeezed gently. Her flesh was aching. *Sensitive.* And it was sensitive because—

Maggie pulled back abruptly. Reality and the present moment eclipsed the lure of the past.

'What are you doing?' Her voice was husky.

'You mean what are *we* doing?'

The full impact of the fact that he was here, and that within about a nanosecond she had been in his arms again, combusting all over, was not welcome. She saw the stamp of very male satisfaction on his face and it incensed her.

She pushed free of Nikos's arms. 'Oh, my God—you're so arrogant you really thought you could just pick up where we left off a year ago? Is this some kind of fetish you have for menial staff—?'

'Stop that.' His voice was like the lash of a whip.

Maggie's skin was hot and tight, her heart hammering. Between her legs she was slick and hot. Her breasts were aching.

But suddenly she remembered and she turned around. 'I have to go. I don't have time to stand here and be mauled by a rich playboy who gets his kicks from—'

'Now, wait just a sec—'

'Maggie, *there* you are. I've been looking all over for you.'

Maggie came to a standstill. There was a young woman standing in the doorway leading into the kitchen, holding a baby in her arms. He had dark hair and dark eyes and his legs and arms were windmilling frantically.

Immediately everything else was forgotten and

Maggie instinctively reached for him, cradling him in her arms, checking him over. 'Is he okay?'

'He's fine—I think he's just hungry. We ran out of your expressed milk.'

Maggie looked at Sara. She was from Merkazad, the country in the Middle East where Nessa's sister lived with her family.

'Okay—thanks, Sara, I'll feed him and put him down. Can you do me a huge favour and let Nessa know I won't be back to the party this evening?'

'Sure. No problem.'

Maggie saw the girl's eyes go behind her and widen as she took in Nikos Marchetti. *Damn.*

Sara left and Maggie slowly turned around. Much as she would have preferred to keep going in the other direction she knew she couldn't.

Her breasts were tingling again, but for entirely different reasons now. If she hadn't been so distracted by this man she would have noticed the signs and gone to her son before he'd had to be brought to her.

Nikos was looking at the baby with a mixture of shock, incomprehension and horror. His bow-tie was askew. Hair mussed.

Had she done that?

Mortification sent a hot wave of shame through her body. She had so much to say to this man, and yet when the moment had come she'd said nothing. Just climbed all over him like a lust-crazed monkey.

She lifted her son and put him over her shoulder, patting his back with an unsteady hand. 'I need to go. I have to feed him.'

She turned, but of course she didn't get far.

'Wait just a minute.'

His accent was thicker, and somehow that made Maggie's heart race again. What was wrong with her? She was in a moment of real crisis and her feverish brain was stuck in a lust loop.

Nikos came and stood in front of her. 'What the hell, Maggie…? Who is this?'

'He's my son. Daniel.'

My son. Her conscience pricked.

Nikos was shaking his head. 'So you had sex with someone else…? Who?'

The fact that he was trying to deny knowledge that he'd been told about her pregnancy sent her hormones into orbit.

'Someone else? Would that have been bad thing? When *you've* undoubtedly had sex with a legion of women in the past year? I don't have time for this—please get out of my way.'

Nikos moved aside without even realising what he was doing. Maggie swept past with the baby on her shoulder. He automatically followed her, in shock.

She'd had a baby. With someone else. She'd slept with someone else right after him—it would have to have been. The baby only looked a few months old.

That realisation curdled in his gut. Along with her accusation that he must have slept with countless women. If only!

The baby's dark eyes regarded Nikos steadily over Maggie's shoulder as she strode back in through the kitchens and up the stairs into the main part of the house.

Nikos was barely aware of staff around them. He felt as if he'd been in an explosion and he couldn't hear properly. Everything was muffled. Distorted.

Suddenly Maggie stopped and turned from the step above him. 'Why are you following me?'

He heard her perfectly, and for the first time he heard the panic in her voice.

He went still inside. She'd attacked him when he'd asked her about the father.

His gaze moved from her to the back of the baby's head. Dark hair. Maggie was fair. His mother had been fair, but his father's darker, stronger genes had won out. He'd had dark hair as a baby. Not that there were many photos of him.

His gaze shifted back to Maggie. She was pale. Something else curdled in his gut now. Suspicion.

'Who is the father, Maggie?'

'I'm not having this conversation here.'

She turned and kept on hurrying up the stairs, entering a corridor on the first floor. Nikos followed her. She went through a door. He stopped on the threshold. It was a spacious bedroom with a cot in the corner. For the baby.

She was looking at him, eyes wide. No longer antagonistic. Hunted.

'Maggie, who is the father?'

'You know you are—why are you asking me as if you don't know?'

Nikos looked at her. It was as if he'd heard her words but they were still hanging in the air between them. Not impacting fully.

He frowned. 'I *know* I am? What are you talking about?'

The baby's back stiffened and he made a mewling sound. Maggie looked distracted. 'I have to feed him. Can you wait outside?' When Nikos didn't move she said, *'Please?'*

Feeling blindsided, Nikos just watched as she came towards him. He stepped back over the threshold and she closed the door in his face. He heard her making comforting sounds as she presumably tended to the baby, baring her breast— the same breast he'd just cupped in a heat haze of lust.

Theos.

He walked away from the door, dazed. He paced down the corridor and back again, one word circling through his mind: *father.*

His only association with the concept of fatherhood was a toxic and complicated thing. His own father had been many things, but a father in the true sense of the word hadn't been one of them. He didn't even know what having a father felt like.

He reeled as the significance of this sank in.

If it was true.

One minute he'd had his hands full of Maggie, feverish with lust, her curves even more delicious than he remembered, and the next he'd been looking at a baby in her arms.

He was back outside the bedroom door now. He could hear Maggie's voice, indistinct, making crooning noises.

Nikos looked around. Nothing but an empty corridor and the woman behind this door with a baby who might or might not be his. And what had she said? Something about *'you know you are'*? That made no sense to him at all.

Nikos looked at the end of the corridor, the stairs leading back downstairs. He heard the muted sounds of the party outside—soft jazz playing, laughter, clinking glasses. The soundtrack to so much of his life up till now. Strangely, though, he didn't feel an urge to escape back to it. He wanted to stay right here and quiz Maggie until what she'd said made sense to him.

Minutes passed and Nikos paced up and down. He felt pressure on his chest. As if someone was sitting on it. Constricting him. He went to loosen his tie but it was already loose.

How long did it take to feed a baby?

When his frustration was about to boil over, Nikos stood outside the door, hand raised, ready to knock. Suddenly it opened and Maggie stood there. Pale. No baby. He looked behind her and could see the shape of the baby in the cot. She'd dimmed the lighting.

She stood back. 'You'd better come in.'

Maggie wished she felt calmer after the shock of seeing Nikos again…kissing him, him seeing the baby…but she didn't. She still felt jittery. It had taken her ages to settle Daniel, because he'd obviously sensed her tension.

Nikos walked in. He looked grim. Maggie directed him to another door which led into a small sitting room. She closed the adjoining door to the bedroom and watched as Nikos prowled around the room like a magnificent caged animal. A panther.

He stopped at the bookshelves, his back to her, hair curling over the back of his jacket. He said, 'You took your books with you.'

She hadn't expected him to notice. Her gut clenched as she remembered that moment last year. 'Yes. They come everywhere with me.'

He turned around. 'Did you leave Kildare House because you were pregnant?'

Maggie shook her head. 'I told you—it was never a long-term plan.'

Nikos gritted his jaw, making it pop. 'How did you end up here, then?'

She swallowed. 'I got to know Nessa Barbier from living in the area. When she heard I was leaving Kildare House she offered me a job here to tide me over…and shortly after I arrived I found out about…about the baby. She insisted I stay. They have a créche here, for the children of their staff. Nessa herself has two children. I worked in the kitchen under the head chef until a few weeks before I gave birth. Then she offered me a deal so I could keep doing some part-time work after the baby was born—they have staff here to mind him. Like this evening…'

Amidst the tension Maggie felt emotional, thinking of how supportive both Nessa and her husband had been. Unlike the man in front of her, who had never contacted her even though—

'You're saying the baby is mine?'

'His name is Daniel, and, yes, he's yours.' The insulting assumption that he might be another man's—that she would have so quickly jumped into bed with another man—hit Maggie anew.

'I never planned on having children.' Nikos said.

Why? Maggie pushed the question aside for now. 'Well, you do have a child.'

'If you're so sure he's my son then why didn't you tell me before now? The moment you fell pregnant?'

The affront made Maggie's spine rigid. She had agonised over whether or not to tell him—especially in light of her experiences with her own father—but ultimately she'd decided that she didn't have the right *not* to tell him, even if that came with the risk of not knowing how he would respond.

'I went to your offices in London—I even checked to see if you'd be there. You didn't leave me a personal number to contact you.'

Nikos frowned. 'I didn't see you.'

'No,' Maggie said, feeling bitter and humiliated all over again. 'Because I didn't get further than your secretary on the top floor.'

'When was this?'

'When I was about six months pregnant. Last February.'

Nikos looked as if he was trying to figure something out. 'What was the secretary's name?'

'Chantelle.'

Maggie would never forget her fake smile and patronising tone. She'd looked pointedly at Maggie's distended belly and told her, *'Oh, no, Mr Marchetti is far too busy to meet with you today, but I'll be sure to pass on your note to him.'*

Maggie said, 'I wrote you a note.' *Like you left me a note.* 'She said she'd pass it on.'

'Well, she didn't.'

Maggie frowned. 'But I saw you with her—I

waited for a while outside your offices, hoping I might catch you leaving—'

She stopped there, recalling how it had felt to see Nikos emerge with the tall, blonde woman who had been everything Maggie hadn't in that moment: slim, elegant, beautiful. Coiffed. They'd disappeared into the back of a sleek car before Maggie had been able to move towards them.

Nikos was shaking his head. 'She didn't give it to me.'

'But...' Maggie absorbed this. She sat down on the small two-seater couch behind her. 'She told me she'd pass it on.'

Nikos unfolded his arms and paced back and forth. He stopped, funnelled a hand through his hair, clearly agitated. 'I fired her around that time.'

'Why?'

'Inappropriate behaviour. She was sending me naked pictures of herself. It doesn't surprise me that she might have suspected we'd had a relationship and gone out of her way to disrupt it.'

'If you can call one night a "relationship",' Maggie muttered.

Nikos either didn't hear her or chose to ignore her comment. 'What did your note say?'

'It said that I was pregnant with your baby and we needed to talk.'

Nikos paced back and forth again. He muttered something that sounded suspiciously rude. Then he stopped and faced her again. 'I used protection that night.'

Maggie's face grew hot. 'I know. It must have failed.'

Nikos was struggling to contain the sheer magnitude of this news and what it potentially meant. 'You could have tried again...once the baby was born.'

'It's all been a bit of a blur since the birth, to be honest.'

Nikos hated to admit it but he could see the faintly purple shadows under her eyes now. And when he thought of how she'd felt in his arms just now... In spite of those curves he could tell she'd lost weight.

But if anything she was more beautiful. It was as if she'd grown into herself in order to embody something earthy and impossibly sensual.

Everything in him resisted her pull on him in the midst of this bombshell. Rejected this news. He did not want a child. Not now—not ever.

Maggie continued, oblivious to Nikos's inner turmoil.

'I didn't try again because I believed that you'd got my note and weren't interested. But I don't regret what happened. I don't regret having Daniel for a second, even though I know it's not what you want.'

The fact that she was echoing his thoughts

wasn't welcome. 'First I need to confirm that he is my son—then I will decide how to proceed.'

Maggie looked hunted. For the first time in his cynical life Nikos had to acknowledge that he suspected Maggie was telling the truth. Not that he should trust her word alone, of course.

And in spite of all of this he was still burningly aware of her. This bombshell hadn't diminished his desire for her one iota. He was afraid he might give in to the impulse to haul her into his arms and kiss her into relaxing the rigid line of her spine...kiss her into apologising for turning his life upside down in the space of a couple of hours.

He needed to leave now. His emotions were too volatile, mixed with an even more volatile desire. He needed to leave before he could do something he would regret.

He said, 'I'll arrange to have a DNA test done as soon as possible. You'll be hearing from me.'

CHAPTER FIVE

NIKOS WAS GONE before Maggie could say another word. She let out a shuddery breath. The sounds of the party were a faint hum in the distance. She wondered if he had gone back to the party. Why wouldn't he? He was a playboy after all. But he hadn't looked like a playboy just now—he'd looked shell-shocked.

Which was about as much as she'd expected. He hadn't said anything about taking responsibility—which was also what she'd expected. It wasn't as if he hadn't been brutally honest.

She just couldn't help feeling sorry for Daniel, who was destined to suffer the same fate she had. No father on the scene.

The fact that he'd never got the note she'd left him had taken some of the fuel out of the anger she'd nurtured over the past few months, and without the anger there was just a sense of disappointment. Which was as dangerous as it was unwelcome.

Once he had confirmation that Daniel was his,

and inevitably left them to get on with their lives as he would his, she would pick up the pieces and tell herself that it was enough that he knew.

In many ways she could handle this—she knew how to deal with an absent and uninterested father. She wouldn't know how to handle Nikos if he actually wanted to be involved. The man came within ten feet of her and she couldn't think straight, so this really was for the best.

Nikos threw back another measure of whiskey, poured from his decanter into a tumbler in his living room at Kildare House. The fact that he was even using a tumbler and not drinking straight from the decanter didn't say much about his level of control, which felt very frayed.

Twenty-four hours ago he'd been blissfully ignorant. Blissfully ignorant of the fact that the woman who had been haunting his X-rated dreams for a year had become a mother in the interim. The mother of his child. Potentially.

It was disconcerting to think of his father's very dominant dark Italian genes appearing in this baby. The only hint Nikos held of his mother was in his hazel-green eyes. Those strong Italian genes had wiped his Greek mother out in more ways than one.

His father had been dark physically and morally, thinking nothing of stripping Nikos's mother of her fortune to further his own ambitions.

When she'd realised that Domenico Marchetti—handsome, charming, ruthless—had only married her to get his hands on the vast Constantinos inheritance she'd killed herself. Nikos had been two, and from that day to this he'd depended solely on himself.

Hence the reason why he'd always vowed not to have children. No way did he want to be responsible for the welfare of an innocent child.

And yet already Nikos could feel a resistance in him to the idea that Daniel might *not* be his son. Which was as shocking as it was unnerving. This was not a scenario he'd ever expected to face. He was the least likely among the three half-brothers to settle down...have a family. And yet if Maggie was to be believed he was well on the way to that situation.

If Maggie was to be believed.

Nikos had seen too much and experienced too much of human nature to trust for a second in a woman he'd spent only one night with, no matter what kind of persona she'd projected. Sweet. Innocent.

He felt a prickling sense of exposure. Had he been played? Spectacularly? A year ago and now? By a woman looking to feather her nest?

Nikos drew out his phone from his pocket and made a couple of calls.

Within a few minutes his phone pinged and he looked at the link that had been sent to him by his security company. He saw grainy CCTV images of Maggie, taken in early February. She could be seen entering his office building, wearing jeans and a coat, her pregnant belly evident. Her hair fell down over her shoulders in wild waves.

Nikos's gut clenched on seeing this evidence of her visit, of her attempt to tell him about her pregnancy. And he felt a pang of regret that he hadn't witnessed her body growing and ripening with his child. Something he had never in a million years expected to experience.

He put away his phone and poured himself another whiskey. But this time it left an acrid taste in his mouth. The truth was, all the whiskey in the world couldn't prepare him for what was coming.

His son would be a Marchetti, with all the baggage that entailed. And, as much as Nikos didn't welcome the thought of a child—had never planned to have a child—he knew one thing: no child of his would ever suffer the abandonment he'd suffered. Or the persistent feeling of standing on the periphery of his own family.

He and his half-brothers had always been kept apart from each other. His older half-brother, Sharif, had grown up mainly in his Arabian mother's country—but as eldest son he'd been groomed by their father to take over from a young age. Nikos's younger brother, Maks, had grown up in Rome, with his Russian mother and younger sister, and as Rome was their paternal ancestral home Nikos had always felt envious of him for having that link to their shared past.

Maks's younger sister had since been proved not to be their father's daughter—not that Nikos had ever had a chance to get to know her anyway...

But that was enough about his brothers and a sister who was not even his sister. If this baby *was* his it would have a claim on the Marchetti legacy through Nikos. And for the first time in his life he felt a sense of destiny and a tangible sense of family that he'd never really had before.

The next day Maggie drove up the drive to Kildare House. She hadn't expected to be back here again and her heart lurched when it was revealed at the top of the drive. She'd always liked this house over any of the other houses her mother had worked in, where they'd inevitably lived either in a gate lodge or in cramped staff quarters.

The first time Maggie had seen it she'd loved it. It was the kind of house she'd always dreamed of living in one day, and living there so long without its owner in residence she'd developed a false sense of ownership.

But then Nikos had arrived. Asserting his ownership of the house. *And her.*

A shiver of memory went through her when she thought of what had happened.

For a while, in the aftermath of that night a year ago, Maggie had blamed grief for the reason why she'd acted so uncharacteristically—jumping into bed with Nikos Marchetti after little more than a brief conversation and some whiskey.

But if she was honest with herself she knew it hadn't been grief at all. Or the alcohol. It had been the man and the seismic effect he'd had on her the moment she'd opened the front door to him for the first time.

Maggie parked the car. She was here to meet with the local doctor and Nikos. The doctor would be taking swabs for a DNA test.

She sucked in a deep breath and got out, extricated Daniel's baby seat. Before she could knock on the front door, though, it opened, and Maggie was surprised to see a middle-aged smiling man, dressed in smart dark trousers and a white shirt.

He said, 'Hello, you must be Miss Taggart. I'm Andrew Wilson, the new housekeeper. It's lovely to meet you—and this must be Daniel?'

Daniel smiled gummily, oblivious to the circumstances.

Then Nikos appeared behind the new housekeeper, and Maggie wasn't prepared to see him.

He said, 'We'll have some tea and coffee in the living room please, Mr Wilson.' He held out a hand to her. 'Here, let me take help you.'

Maggie was tempted to insist that she could manage, but that felt petty. As she handed over the baby seat she noticed how Nikos was careful not to look too closely at Daniel.

He led the way to the living room, turning around. 'Where should I put him?'

Maggie came over and took the baby seat from him, placing it safely on top of a table so she could keep an eye on Daniel.

She looked around. For a moment the sense of déjà-vu was almost overwhelming. Even though it was bright outside and not dusky night, the scene was acutely familiar.

Nikos glanced at his watch. 'The doctor will be arriving any minute. She'll take swabs for the DNA tests.'

Maggie bit her lip. Anyone with eyes could see that Daniel was this man's son. But of course he'd need proof.

'What then?' she asked.

'Then we wait for the results. And then…depending on the outcome…we discuss what we do.'

'He's your son.'

'I can't afford to trust you on your word alone. Too much is at stake.'

Anger at herself for having succumbed to the charms of such a man—the kind who didn't trust and who demanded DNA tests—made her say caustically, 'Well, the feeling is mutual. I don't trust you either.'

'You trusted me enough to let me be your first lover,' he supplied silkily.

Maggie flushed all over. 'That was a moment of flawed judgement.'

He arched a brow. 'That was chemistry, pure and simple. Don't tell me you're still holding out for your boring hero?'

Maggie squirmed. She'd told him so much. *Too* much.

At that moment the doorbell chimed. Within a minute Mr Wilson was showing the doctor into the living room.

Maggie welcomed the distraction, getting Daniel out of his seat.

The procedure was done with the minimum of fuss and within minutes the doctor stood up. 'It'll take a couple of days for the results to come back. I'll let you know as soon as I have them.'

Nikos saw the doctor out and Maggie patted Daniel's back absently. Everything was about to change irrevocably. Nikos came back and she turned around to face him. She noticed that he was looking at Daniel. For the first time she had to appreciate what a shock this must be for him.

Impulsively she said, 'I'm sorry that you found out like this. But I did try to tell you.'

He lifted his gaze to hers. 'I know.'

'You know? How?'

'I got my security team to check the cameras and someone has been in touch with Chantelle.

She confirmed it.' Nikos shook his head. 'She did a lot of damage.'

Maggie shrugged minutely. 'It's okay. You know now…or you will know soon.'

Nikos looked at his watch, suddenly business-like. 'I have to go to London for some meetings. I'll come back when I have confirmation that he's mine.'

The abruptness with which he was going to leave again made Maggie feel a little winded. She had no doubt that if Daniel should prove not to be his baby she wouldn't see him again. What-ever passion had blazed between them was well and truly snuffed out. But Daniel *was* his, and she would have to see him again and accept the consequences of her actions.

Nikos followed her out to the car and Maggie noticed him looking at Daniel again for a long moment through the window. She couldn't help asking, 'Did you really never want to have chil-dren?'

He stood back and looked away from Daniel to her. 'The short, brutal answer? No. But if he is mine I will accept him fully and things will be very different.'

He turned to walk back inside and Maggie said, 'Wait just a second. What does that mean?'

He came and stood close. Hands on his hips. She sensed volatile emotions under the surface and to her mortification shivers of awareness ran through her blood, recalling his volatility a year ago.

He said, 'It means exactly what I said: if he's mine, rest assured that I will not shirk my responsibility.'

Three days later

Maggie walked into the plush Dublin city centre hotel. One of the city's oldest, and situated on St Stephen's Green, it oozed timeless elegance and sophistication. She'd been delivered here in a chauffeur-driven SUV—summoned by Nikos Marchetti.

The spurt of rebellion she'd felt earlier, when preparing to come and meet Nikos, had galvanised her to dress down for the occasion. But now that felt like teenage theatrics. She'd be surprised if she wasn't thrown out on her ear before she even reached the reception desk.

But no one stopped her. In fact a suited manager approached her and said, 'Miss Taggart?'

How did they know?

Maggie nodded. He smiled. 'Please…let me show you to Mr Marchetti's suite.'

Maggie dutifully followed him into a rococo decorated lift and her stomach dropped as they ascended. She really wasn't prepared for whatever was going to come next. But she couldn't go back now.

The manager led her out of the lift, down a luxuriously carpeted corridor to a room at the end. A light rap on the door and it opened almost immediately.

Nikos looked serious. Shirtsleeves rolled up, hair mussed. Dark trousers. His dark gaze swept her up and down.

'Maggie.'

'Nikos.'

The air was charged. Thick with sudden tension and filled with an awareness that she did not welcome because it was one-sided.

The manager cleared his throat. 'Can I send some refreshments up?'

Nikos didn't take his eyes off Maggie. 'Just some tea and coffee.'

Maggie looked at the manager. 'Thank you.'

He left and Nikos stood back, holding the door open. Maggie tried not to breathe in his scent as she passed him, but it filtered through anyway, precipitating dangerous memories.

She went straight over to one of the windows overlooking the green park. The suite was vast. She caught a glimpse of a bedroom…rumpled sheets. She felt hot.

'Where's Daniel?'

Maggie's heart hitched. *Daniel.* He knew he was his son now.

She turned around. 'The Barbiers' nanny, Sara, is minding him. I expressed some milk.'

She didn't know why she felt defensive. But it was as if now that he had confirmation of Daniel's parentage Nikos thought he had a right to ask her questions about him. About her. About her mothering. Would Nikos even know what expressing milk was?

He gestured to a couch. 'Please, sit down.'

He stood with legs apart, every inch the bristling Alpha male. A million miles from the teasing seductive playboy who'd turned her world upside down in one night.

Maggie swallowed. 'It's okay. I'm comfortable standing.'

He folded his arms. 'So, when *would* you have told me about Daniel? Would you have waited until he was walking and talking before you got around to it?'

No beating around the bush. Now he knew for sure, and he was angry. A muscle pulsed in his jaw. She was surprised at the emotion—she hadn't expected it. She hadn't expected a lot about this man, though, and he consistently surprised her.

She had to be honest. 'I don't know. I believed you knew but weren't interested. I guess I might have tried again when Daniel was a bit older.'

He paced back and forth, energy crackling. He stopped and faced her. 'I know it's not entirely your fault, but while your low opinion of me is refreshing, when I'm usually surrounded by sycophants, I can't believe that if I hadn't turned up at the Barbier party I might easily have missed out on a year of my son's life? Two years? More? As it is I have missed the birth of my own son. His first few months.'

Anger spiked at his accusatory tone. 'All you left me a year ago was a note—not even a personal number. You couldn't have made it clearer to me that you weren't interested in anything beyond that one night. And now you expect me to believe that you would have been interested in the minutiae of the birth of a baby you didn't believe was yours? You really don't have to pretend to be interested now. It's just us here. I know how this goes. My father—'

Nikos's voice was like a whip. 'Your father? What's *he* got to do with this?'

Maggie cursed her runaway mouth again. But it was too late. 'My father was rich—very rich. He had an affair with my mother and when she fell pregnant he denied all knowledge. Threatened her into staying away. He had no desire to be a father or to share any of his fortune.'

Nikos arched a brow. He'd never looked more imperious. 'And that pertains to me how? Because I'm rich too?'

'That and the fact that you told me specifically that you're not into relationships or families.'

His brow lowered. 'Well, that was before I had a son.'

A shiver went through her—a sense that once again Nikos was going to do the opposite of what she expected.

On impulse, she asked, 'Why didn't you want a relationship or children? Was it because you lost your mother?'

Nikos was so full of conflicting emotions and so full of desire for the woman in front of him that it was hard to think straight. Even though she was dressed like a hippy. Wearing worn dungarees and a singlet vest. Sandals. Hair up in an untidy knot.

She looked as if she'd just come from serving up lunch at an ashram. And yet he'd never seen anything sexier. It incensed him. He needed his wits about him, and all he wanted to do was carry her into the bedroom and spread her on the bed for his delectation.

Desire was a heavy, hot knot inside him, but he forced himself to focus. He debated giving Maggie some platitude, but for some reason he felt the urge to be brutally honest.

'I never intended to have children because I didn't want any child of mine to go through what I did.'

'What *did* you go through?'

His skin prickled. He would never entertain such questions from anyone else—much less a woman he had slept with—but this situation demanded a different response. She deserved to know what she was getting into.

'My mother killed herself when I was two—driven to it by my father, who had married her only for her inheritance. She believed he loved her. Soon after she died he married again, and his new wife had no interest in taking on his dead wife's son, so I was sent to live with my grandparents in Greece. They never forgave me for my mother's sins—for running off with her Italian lover and giving him her fortune. When I was old enough to be of some use my father took me away from Greece and sent me to boarding school in England. I was moved around like a pawn. A poor little rich boy who rebelled as a means of getting his father's attention. To no avail.'

Maggie's eyes had widened and were now full of something that Nikos had never seen before. Genuine emotion. It impacted on him in a way that made him feel on edge.

She said, 'I'm sorry you went through that.'

'Don't be. It did me a favour. I learned early on that the only person you can count on is yourself.'

Nikos saw the shimmer of moisture in Maggie's eyes and reacted instinctively, needing to take that emotion out of her. 'Don't do that—don't look at me like that.'

'Like what?' asked Maggie.

What he'd just told her had torn down some

vital defence, leaving her exposed, vulnerable. She'd also learnt not to trust anyone outside of herself and her mother from an early age. Her father, who should have been one of the most important people in her life, had also let her down badly.

Nikos said now, 'I'm not a very nice person, Maggie. Don't look at me like you care. Do you know what's on my mind right now? How much I want you.'

Maggie's thoughts skittered to a halt. *He wanted her.* She felt breathless. Tight inside.

'You...? Even now, with the baby...?'

He nodded. 'I've wanted you for a year. Only you. I told you—you haunted me.'

You haunted me.

Maggie's mind was melting. She didn't believe him.

'You're just saying that.'

Nikos looked imperious again. 'Why would I lie?'

He moved closer. The air thickened. Suddenly Maggie couldn't recall what they'd been talking about. It didn't seem important...

Nikos reached out and cupped her jaw, moving a thumb across her lower lip. Little fires raced across her skin and an intense longing made her sway closer.

Now he was so close that she could smell him. Their bodies were almost touching. Every pulse point was going crazy, making her head light. She was sensitive all over. *He wanted her.* The sharp lance of relief should have shamed her, but it didn't.

'I need to know that you want this too,' he said.

Nikos's blunt demand struck right to her core. Did any woman *not* want him? Impossible. Could he not see how she hungered for him, even though she wished she didn't? She couldn't think straight…she could only say what she felt.

'Yes.'

She had a moment of déjà vu. Thought back to that first night when he'd asked her if she wanted him. Made sure of it.

The past and the present were meshing. So when he snaked an arm around her waist and pulled her all the way into his body, and she felt her softer curves moulding to his far steelier strength, she had no other thought in her head except, *Yes, please.*

His mouth touched hers and she fell into his kiss like a starving woman, tongue tangling with his, teeth nipping at the firm contour of his lower lip. He surrounded her with a heat and an intensity that thrilled her to her very core.

That she craved.

That she'd missed.

He pulled back. She was panting, but she didn't care. His eyes glittered and his cheeks were flushed. His hands were on the straps of her dungarees, undoing them so that the front fell down. Maggie didn't even have time to think about the fact that she was wearing a breastfeeding bra, because Nikos was pulling up her top and baring her to his hungry gaze.

'*Theos*, Maggie, I have dreamt of this...of you.'

He undid her bra at the front and it sprang open. He took her breasts in his hands, thumbs moving back and forth across nipples sensitive enough to make her gasp. All she could see was his broad chest in front of her—still covered up. She needed to see him...to feel the heat of his skin against hers.

She reached for his buttons, undoing them. Volatile emotions swirled inside her, making her feel reckless like he'd made her feel a year ago, helping her justify making love to him.

But this wasn't last year, this was now. A year later. Not past—*present*.

Realisation hit and her hands stopped.

Daniel.

She dislodged his hands, dragged her dungarees top back up to cover her breasts. 'Wait...we shouldn't be doing this.'

Nikos looked at her, hair ruffled, cheeks lined with colour, eyes glittering. 'It's inevitable whenever we're in close proximity, Maggie.'

His shirt was half open, and even now her hands itched to reach out and touch the part of his chest that was bared.

She shook her head, even though every cell in her body protested at the interruption. 'The last time we did this I got pregnant.'

Nikos felt dazed, drunk with lust, but her words cut through the fog of desire.

Maggie took another step back and he had to curb the reflex to reach out and tug her back. *Christos,* what did this woman do to him? He struggled to regain control, cool his blood. But it was hard when her breasts were all but falling out of her clothes and her face was flushed.

'You're right—this isn't the time or place.'

His voice came out harsh and he saw how she winced. His conscience pricked but he turned around and did up his own clothes. This was not him. He was usually in control. Almost detached from proceedings. He never lost it so much that he seduced housekeepers and got them pregnant—

He cursed again.

He turned around when he had done up his shirt and tucked it in. He battled to cool his libido, but it was next to impossible while Maggie stood only a few feet away, clothed again but no less sexy for it.

The urge to throw caution to the wind and haul her back into his arms and finish what they'd started was overwhelming.

He resisted it.

'I hadn't intended that. I did intend just to talk.'

Eventually she said, 'I... Okay.'

He was more sophisticated than this. What *was* it about this woman that short-circuited his brain and sent it straight to his pants?

He raised his gaze to her flushed face and her wild hair—tumbling around her shoulders now. Her eyes were bright blue and full of things that still made his skin prickle uncomfortably. It was those eyes and the emotion that he'd seen in them that had made him want to turn it into something else.

Passion. Not emotion. He could handle passion.

She was looking at him warily now. He reacted against her silent accusation.

'What just happened was mutual, Maggie.'

Maggie was struggling to regain a sense of composure but it was hard. Those last few cataclysmic minutes in Nikos's arms had flayed a layer of skin off her body. The knowledge that he still wanted her thrummed through her body like a drug, giving her an illicit high.

But that wasn't why she was here.

'We need to talk about what happens next,' she said.

Nikos folded his arms across his chest. 'Yes, we do need to talk. Now I know that Daniel is mine we can move forward.'

'What does that mean?'

The dark gold and green lights in his eyes glinted. 'Marriage, Maggie. It means we need to marry.'

CHAPTER SIX

OF ALL THE things Maggie had been expecting, she'd never—

She stared at Nikos, wondering if she'd heard right. 'Did you really just say *marry?*'

Nikos nodded, watching her carefully.

Maggie's legs felt suspiciously rubbery, but she locked them in order to stay standing. 'That's the most ridiculous thing I've ever heard. We barely know each other.'

Nikos's mouth firmed. 'And yet we've shared an intimacy that has resulted in a child. Some would say that constitutes knowing one another just fine. People in other cultures marry for a lot less.'

Maggie felt shaky. Panicky.

Seizing desperately onto anything to try and make him see sense, she asked, 'Is this what you want? Really? When you've told me what happened to you?'

There was a long moment of silence, and then Nikos said tightly, 'It's because of what happened to me that I'm determined to be there for my son. My father failed my mother and me—I won't do that to you or my son.'

Shock reverberated through Maggie as she absorbed this. She wasn't sure what was worse: a father who didn't want anything to do with them or a father who would take responsibility out of a sense of duty and nothing more?

'Do we need to get married, though? Can't we just come to some agreement?'

'There's more at stake than just us.'

She frowned. 'What are you talking about?'

'The Marchetti Group. Even though some time has passed since my father's death, people are still watching to see how us three half-brothers will work as a cohesive unit. We're all single, which makes us inherently less trustworthy to our largely conservative shareholders who are growing more nervous as the years pass. Stability of the brand and its image is everything.'

His mouth twisted.

'When the press find out about you and Daniel they'll have a field-day. It won't come as a huge surprise to many that I've fathered a child, but it will make the shareholders even more nervous.'

Maggie shelved his comment about people not being surprised. 'So you want us to get married purely to shore up the image of the Marchetti brand?'

'It won't just be for that—although that is a big part of it, yes.'

Panic threatened to rise again. Nikos sounded so implacable. Her mind raced, trying to take this in.

'But I don't know anything about you...' The memory of looking him up on the internet made her blush. Quickly she said, 'I mean, what about your family? You have two brothers? Are you even close?'

Nikos's face turned to stone. 'I have two *half*-brothers—one older, one younger. We all have different mothers. And in a word? No, we're not especially close. But we're all committed to the Marchetti Group.'

That sounded so...*cold*.

In as reasonable a tone as Maggie could muster, she said, 'I understand why you want to do things differently—so do I—but you of all people know the damage a bad marriage can do. We don't love each other.'

Nikos's face became derisive. 'Love? If anything can destabilise a marriage it's love. Love is for naive fools.'

'It's not naive to believe in love.' Her hands balled into fists at her sides. 'I loved my mother and she loved me. She did everything to protect me. It almost killed me when she died. And when Daniel was born...the love I felt for him straight away is like nothing I can describe. All-encompassing. I would do anything for him.'

Nikos heard Maggie's words, but she might as well have been speaking another language. He had no idea what she was talking about. He didn't dispute her feelings, but he'd never felt anything like what she was describing.

When his grandparents had died he'd felt nothing. They'd bitterly disapproved of him and had always seen him as evidence of their daughter's foolishness. They'd let his father take him away when he'd turned twelve without even sparing him a backward glance.

He didn't have to be a psychologist to know that a lot of his rebellion had been as much to do with testing the boundaries—seeing what it would take to get him expelled from the family completely—as it had with getting his father's attention. And, if he was honest, his half-brothers' attention too.

But Nikos didn't welcome this introspection, and he had a sense that Maggie was seeing far too much.

'You say you'd do anything for our son? I can offer you and Daniel a secure and stable life. A luxurious life. That's more of a guarantee than love will ever give you.'

Maggie's teeth worried at her lower lip and Nikos had to curb his urge to reach out and tug it free. The waves of desire that had beat so furiously just a short while before were still there… just under the surface.

'We have something far more potent and tangible than love between us. Desire. And a child.'

'Desire won't last for ever, though…and then what?'

Nikos didn't have an answer for that, and it irritated him intensely. He usually had no problem getting people to agree to whatever he proposed.

Maggie spoke again. 'This is a lot to think about.'

Frustration at how off-centre she made him feel made Nikos's voice sharp. 'You've had a year to think about it.'

She paled and he felt a stab of conscience. *You should have tried harder to find her.*

He pushed the inner voice down and forced a more conciliatory tone into his own voice. 'I think we can do better for Daniel. He deserves better.'

'You've barely looked at him.'

Nikos's chest constricted when he thought of that tiny vulnerable body. That dark hair.

'I have no experience with babies. It'll take me some time to adjust.'

Maggie couldn't say anything to that. He was right. She'd had a year to adjust to being a mother. She'd had the experience of carrying Daniel inside her. Giving birth to him. Bonding with him instantly. Even though motherhood still terrified her, she'd found it an easier adjustment than she'd expected.

But what Nikos was suggesting was a quantum leap into a dimension she'd never considered.

'If I did agree to marry you how would it work, exactly?' she asked.

'I think five years would be enough time to give a lasting impression of stability and create a secure base for our son. Then we can come to an arrangement about custody.'

Five years.

Maggie felt breathless. 'And where would we go...where would we live? I don't even know where you're based.'

'I'm mainly based in Paris, but I have apartments in New York, London and Athens. My apartment in Paris overlooks the Eiffel Tower.'

The perfect location for an international playboy.

Maggie felt a bubble of hysteria threatening to rise. Worse, she could still feel the imprint of Nikos's mouth on hers. Hot and demanding. He might have implied that he hadn't slept with anyone else since he'd slept with her, but she'd be naive in the extreme to believe that.

'Can I think about this?' she asked.

Maggie could see the struggle on Nikos's face. Evidently he wasn't used to not being given answers in the affirmative straight away. Well, tough.

'You can—but we don't have much time before the press sniff around and find out what's going on. What I'd like is for you and Daniel to leave with me when I return to Paris tomorrow afternoon.'

Maggie felt winded. 'Daniel doesn't even have a passport.'

Nikos waved a hand. 'I can arrange all the travel documents. We'll be flying privately, which makes things easier. Things move fast in my world. The sooner we can contain and manage this situation, the better.'

So she and Daniel were a *situation*?

Any vaguely romantic notions Maggie had entertained about meeting a nice, kind, dependable man were truly incinerated by now.

Feeling a little shell-shocked, she said, 'I need to get back to Daniel. And I need to think about all of this…'

To her relief, Nikos went to the suite door and opened it. She felt so raw after that kiss and the ensuing conversation that she knew if he touched her again she would have had no defences in place at all.

He said to her, on the threshold, 'You know what's best for our son.'

She looked at Nikos. She did—that was the problem. And the other problem was that she didn't trust herself around Nikos, and agreeing to his plan would put them in close proximity, and close proximity spelled danger, because everything was turned on its head now and she was facing a scenario she had no idea how to navigate.

Marriage.

As if reading the turmoil in her head, Nikos said, 'I have yours and Daniel's best interests at heart. You'll be a very wealthy woman for the rest of your life, and life with me won't be boring—I can guarantee you that.'

Oh, she was sure it wouldn't be boring. Every second with this man was a rollercoaster of emotions and sensations.

'Maybe I *want* boring,' she said.

That cynical look came into Nikos's eyes. 'Then I'd have to say it's too late. You made a choice last year and you didn't choose *boring* then, did you?'

No, she hadn't chosen boring last year. She'd jumped into the fire and got burned in the process.

In the end Maggie knew she didn't really have a choice. She'd expected Nikos to want to have nothing to do with them—in fact that would almost have been easier, in some perverse way.

Because he affects you.

And not just that, Maggie thought, feeling guilty, but because it was what she knew.

But more importantly there was Daniel. And the fact that Daniel's grounding years could be spent with two parents—together. Giving him a start in life that neither Maggie nor Nikos had had.

How could she argue with that?

She'd called Nikos late last night and told him over the phone that she would agree to marry him.

There'd been a beat, and then he'd said in a deep voice, 'You're making the right decision, Maggie.'

His car had picked her and Daniel and their paltry belongings up earlier that morning.

It had proved surprisingly easy to extricate herself from the life she'd built at the Barbiers' stud. Which had been a reminder of how her mother had picked up and moved with each new job, and a reminder that Maggie wanted more for her son.

She knew she had to live with the consequences of her actions. Yesterday in that hotel suite had been an example of how little control she had around Nikos. She'd all but thrown herself at him. Seduced by his sheer charisma. By his power.

Like mother like daughter.

She resisted the snarky voice.

'Are you comfortable enough?'

Maggie's head jerked around. She'd been watching Dublin drop away beneath the private plane, still reeling from the sense of just how different her life was going to be.

It had hit her when they'd arrived at a private airfield and she'd seen the gleaming black jet inscribed with the Marchetti Group logo. And when she'd seen the plush cream leather interior. Solicitous staff had offered Maggie everything from tea and coffee to champagne.

Now they were in this luxurious bubble high above the world and Maggie wondered if she'd ever touch the ground again.

'What's going on in that head of yours, Maggie?' asked Nikos. 'I can't read you and it makes me nervous.'

'And you can read everyone else?' she asked, in an effort to deflect him.

His mouth tipped up on one side. 'I'm an excellent poker player.'

Maggie wondered if his ability to read people had been born out of growing up in a relatively hostile environment, surrounded by people who didn't care for him. She hated that it had an impact on her, because Nikos seemed immune to needing *anyone*.

'What if Daniel doesn't want to be heir to a fortune?' Maggie asked, feeling a little desperate as this new reality sank in and thinking of her tiny, vulnerable son.

'Would you deny him his heritage?'

She opened her mouth and shut it again. Of

course she wouldn't deny him. 'It doesn't matter to me if he doesn't have a fortune. It only matters if he's happy and healthy.'

Nikos's mouth firmed. 'A noble thought, but not very realistic. Think of the opportunities I can provide our son.'

Our son.

Maggie looked at Nikos. Even like this, lounging in his seat, he oozed barely leashed energy. His face was stamped with generations of arrogance and pride. He was from a long line of men who were used to being obeyed.

She desperately wanted to see him show some kind of emotion for Daniel. To have some inkling that he wasn't viewing him like some abstract object.

She said, 'I'm not interested in marriage if you're not going to be a father to Daniel. All the stability and security in the world can't protect him from a father who doesn't love him. I don't know if I can trust you to do that.'

Nikos's gaze flicked briefly to Daniel, where he lay in Maggie's arms. An expression she couldn't decipher passed so quickly across his face that it was gone before she could wonder what it was, or why she'd felt it like a soft blow to her belly. She wondered if she should have been so blunt... But surely Nikos Marchetti was cynical down to the deepest part of his marrow...

Wasn't he?

* * *

Nikos didn't like the sensation that Maggie could see right inside him to where he had his own doubts about whether or not he was capable of being the kind of father he'd never had himself. All he knew was that the thought of not being in his son's life made his chest tight.

He said, 'I didn't know until a few days ago that I even had a son. I think you owe me the benefit of the doubt as I try to have a relationship with him. The last thing I want to do is cause him harm.'

Maggie's cheeks pinkened. 'I guess that's fair enough.'

It struck Nikos then that he was renowned for brokering huge deals with the most recalcitrant people in the world—and yet here, with Maggie, even that grudging concession felt like a massive victory.

The thought that he'd met his match in more ways than one made him edgy.

The seat belt bell pinged, indicating that it was okay to get up and move around, and Maggie undid her belt, and the one clipped around the baby, and stood up.

'I'll go into the back and feed and change Daniel.'

Nikos watched her walk down the aisle of the plane, Daniel safely in the crook of her arm. He wasn't unaware of the irony that not so long ago it would have been a very different scenario for him on a jet like this—featuring him and a woman, sometimes even two, unencumbered by anything but the mutual desire to lose themselves for a brief moment.

Because that was all it had been—a brief moment of respite from his ever-present sense of rootlessness and dissatisfaction. And those moments had never filled him with anything but an aftertaste of ennui.

Sleeping with Maggie hadn't felt like that.

No. She'd lingered on his body and his brain for months. Making him ache.

She was the woman he wanted. And she was the mother of his child.

When he'd found her at the Barbiers' stud he'd had no idea about the secret she kept. *His son.* But he was nothing if not skilled at adapting.

He'd learnt young not to expect people to accept him or want him. But he knew Maggie's reluctance for this marriage would turn to acquiescence when she saw the life he could provide for her and his son.

'When you said "apartment", I assumed you meant an actual apartment—not an apartment in a hotel.'

Maggie was standing at the wall of a terrace at the top of an ornate baroque building looking out at the Eiffel Tower. It was so close she could almost touch it.

She'd only been to Paris once before, on a school trip. She couldn't quite believe she was here, in this sophisticated and beautiful city.

Ireland had been enjoying an unnaturally warm summer, but this heat was on another level. A trickle of sweat pooled between her breasts and at her lower back as she looked at people strolling on the plaza near the Eiffel Tower wearing little sundresses and eating ice-cream. She was envious.

'Everyone local leaves Paris in August,' Nikos had told her as they'd driven into the city. 'They'll return over the next few days and the city will come back to life after the *vacances*.' He'd gestured to the crowds thronging the wide boulevards. 'These are all tourists,' he'd said, in a tone that signified disdain.

Maggie had been too distracted by the exquisite architecture, the tall and majestic buildings...

Nikos came and stood beside her now. 'All my apartments are in hotels that we own. The MG Hotel Group. I've found it more...convenient.'

Maggie looked at him, glad of the sunglasses hiding her eyes. 'You own this hotel?'

He nodded.

She should have guessed. When they'd arrived Nikos had been fawned over like visiting royalty.

She thought of something. 'So the house in Ireland—that's the only house you own?'

If she hadn't been looking at him she might

have missed the flicker of an expression she couldn't decipher across his face, the slight tension in his body.

But he sounded nonchalant when he said, 'Yes. Like I said, I bought it when I thought I might invest in horseracing.'

Maggie sensed he was being evasive and wondered why her question had pushed a button for him...

But now he stood back and said, 'Let me show you around.'

Maggie followed Nikos back into the apartment. Daniel was asleep in his baby seat, so she left him where he was. It was much cooler in here, with the air-conditioning.

She tried not to let her jaw drop as Nikos showed her the vast apartment. The gleaming state-of-the-art kitchen had her hands itching to try out the ovens.

She said, 'I suppose you don't use this room much?'

'No. I'm not ashamed to admit I just about know how to boil an egg and that's it. I'm certainly not at your level of proficiency. That's all Mathilde's domain.'

'Mathilde?'

'The housekeeper here. She looks after a couple of the apartments and lives in one herself. She comes and goes. You'll meet her tomorrow. There are some prepared meals in the fridge.'

Maggie made a note to explore later, following Nikos again as he led her through a media room and into a long corridor with rooms off each side. His office, a gym with a lap pool, and then the bedrooms.

He opened a door, letting her precede him. 'This is yours and Daniel's suite.'

She avoided his eye, stepping inside. She wasn't sure what she had expected, but she told herself she was relieved she had her own space. There was a small room for Daniel beside hers, an en suite bathroom and a walk-in wardrobe. Empty at the moment.

He was leaning against the doorframe. 'I've never shared my bedroom with a woman, and even though we'll be married I think it best that we have our own space.'

Maggie kept her expression carefully neutral. 'That's fine—I'd prefer that.'

And she told herself she meant it, even though she felt a little hollow inside. Of *course* a man like Nikos would feel stifled by something as domestic as sharing a bedroom with his wife.

He straightened up from the door. 'After you meet the stylists tomorrow they'll stock up your wardrobe.'

Maggie felt self-conscious. 'I have clothes.'

He responded smoothly. 'I know, but you'll be expected to dress to a certain…*standard*—and naturally I don't expect you to pay for that. Plus you'll need evening dresses for functions like the one we're going to tomorrow night.'

That stung—but what had she expected? Nikos owned part of the world's largest luxury conglomerate. Of course she'd have to look a certain way.

And then she thought of what he'd just said. 'Wait…what function?'

'It's a gala charity event—we'll use it as an opportunity to appear in public as an engaged couple for the first time.'

Suddenly Maggie felt insecure. 'I don't think I'm going to fit into this world very well.'

Nikos took her in: the plaid shirt, the worn jeans. Her hair up in a haphazard knot, with tendrils falling down. No make-up. Scuffed sneakers. Yet still she managed to exert a pull on his libido that was unprecedented. Not even her scruffy attire could hide her very natural beauty.

'You'll fit in just fine with a little polish. I've already released a statement announcing our engagement and the fact that we have a son, so the news is out. We were already papped on the way in here. Impossible to escape them in Paris.'

Maggie had the sensation of a net closing around her. 'Why didn't you tell me you were doing that?'

Nikos looked perplexed for a moment—and then Maggie understood.

She answered for him. 'Because you're not used to deferring to anyone else. Well, for starters, you can inform *me* of anything that affects me or Daniel before you tell the rest of the world.'

Nikos looked unrepentant as he said, 'Then I should probably inform you that I've arranged for us to be married next week by special licence.'

Well, she'd asked for that.

Her legs felt suspiciously weak. 'When did you organise all this?'

'Yesterday after you left the hotel and while we were on the plane.'

She absorbed this.

'Maggie?' he said.

She looked at him, feeling as if things were spinning out of her control. 'I know I've agreed to marry you—I just hadn't expected things to move this fast. Why does it need to happen so quickly?'

Nikos's mouth firmed. 'Because image is everything in this world, and the sooner we put out a united front, with Daniel, the sooner any speculation or gossip will die down.'

'Image is everything in *your* world, you mean,' she pointed out tartly.

'It's your world now, too. Yours and Daniel's.'

She seized on something. 'I can't go to this function with you—what about Daniel?'

'I've arranged for some nannies to come tomorrow morning for you to interview. You'll have to get used to leaving him.'

The speed at which Nikos was turning their

lives upside down made Maggie feel panicky. 'I'll only leave Daniel if I feel I can trust someone.'

Nikos looked as if he was about to argue, but then he said, 'Fair enough.'

As if on cue there was a cry from the sitting room. Maggie welcomed the distraction from their disturbing conversation and hurried back to the main living room. It was more like a vast luxurious waiting room, with big modern canvases on the walls and low glass coffee tables covered with big books featuring photos of beautiful people, beautiful houses, beautiful scenery.

Nikos had followed her into the room and stood near the open French doors leading out to the terrace, watching as she tended to Daniel, settled him to feed.

She suddenly stopped and looked up. 'Is it okay to feed him in here?'

'Of course. This is your home now too, Maggie.'

She privately wondered if he'd still say that if he knew that Daniel might quite easily upchuck all over the expensive fabrics, but the baby was restless, fussing, and she needed to feed him. He latched on with unerring accuracy, making her wince slightly.

'Does it hurt?'

Maggie looked up again. She'd preserved her modesty by placing a muslin cloth over Daniel's head and her breast, but she still felt as if Nikos could see right through it.

She was surprised at his question. 'No, not really—I've been lucky. Some women can't breast-feed at all. But it's just…a little sensitive.'

He said, 'You should make a list of things you need for Daniel and I'll give it to an assistant.'

Maggie nodded, but she was distracted by her view of Nikos, with the backdrop of Paris behind him. She could just see the top of the Eiffel Tower. He had his hands on his hips and he couldn't have looked less domesticated. He looked like what he was: a titan of industry with all the natural attributes of a sex god.

Fresh panic hit her at the thought of how easily he affected her and at the enormity of living this new life.

'We don't have to stay here, you know. I'm happy to stay somewhere else with Daniel. It's a bit grand for us.'

Nikos's gaze narrowed on Maggie. He'd caught a glimpse of voluptuous breast before she'd started to feed the baby, and even that very *un*-inflammatory view had sent his blood spiralling downwards.

He cursed her silently for the ability she had to reduce him to some sort of horny teenager.

She was looking at him, waiting for a response to what she'd said. Either she was the world's greatest actress or she really was something he couldn't understand—an unmercenary person.

But then his cynical reflexes kicked back into gear... No matter what happened between them, she was made for life.

The insidious thought that she might prefer to avail herself of his wealth but not have to spend time with him was rejected outright. She wanted him. He knew that much. And she knew they would have to put on a united front.

A memory assailed him before he could push it away. His father, visiting him in Athens at his grandparents' house when he'd been about eight. Nikos had asked why he couldn't return to Paris with him, and his father had replied, 'I have a new family there. You're better here with Mama's family. You want for nothing—don't be greedy, boy.'

After he'd left Nikos had watched the empty driveway for a long time, with an ache in his chest and a tight throat, wondering what it was about him that made everyone want to push him away...

A chill wind skated over his skin and Nikos pushed the memory down deep. It was a long time since he'd thought of those days. He'd become expert at insulating himself against them with a lot of noise and activity to drown them out.

He folded his arms across his chest, noting how Maggie's eyes darted to his biceps. A shard of lust went to his groin and he welcomed it as an antidote to that memory.

'You've agreed to be my wife,' he said. 'We live together, not apart.'

Maggie expertly switched Daniel to the other breast without revealing any flesh. She said, 'I'm just saying that we don't need all this...'

'It comes with the territory, I'm afraid. You'll get used to it.'

She couldn't *not* get used to it. It was human nature. He almost lamented the fact that he was going to corrupt her.

You started her corruption a year ago, pointed out a voice.

Maggie's head was bent towards the baby, her hand cradling his head. Something about the image made an ache form in Nikos's chest. He didn't even realise he was so fixated until she lifted the baby up and placed him on her shoulder, patting his back.

Daniel emitted a loud burp and Nikos frowned. 'Is he okay?'

Maggie smiled. 'Totally normal. He needs to be winded after he feeds so that air doesn't get trapped in his belly.'

He saw that Daniel had a little bald patch on the back of his head—presumably from where he lay on it. The baby simultaneously terrified him and intrigued him. He had no frame of reference as to how to feel about a baby, a child. His half-brothers were single, like him. Every time he looked at Daniel he felt a curious mix of terror, protectiveness, and some emotion he couldn't name.

Maggie had done herself up again and stood up, Daniel cradled in her arms. She saw him looking at Daniel. 'You should hold him,' she said.

Nikos looked at her in horror. *Hold him?* This tiny vulnerable thing? He wanted to turn and run in the other direction but knew he was being ridiculous. It was a baby. Not a bomb.

The innate confidence that Nikos had taken for granted most of his life was suddenly in short supply. Maggie was looking at him with those big eyes, seeing his vacillation. He couldn't *not* hold his baby—how hard could it be?

'How do I…?'

Maggie came closer. Her scent tickled his nostrils, but not even that could distract him right now.

'Here, crook your arm…make sure his head is supported.'

She placed Daniel onto his arm and his other hand came up instinctively, to hold him from the bottom. The first thing that impacted on him was the solid weight of his son. He hadn't expected him to be so heavy.

Daniel looked up at him with steady, dark long-lashed eyes. Totally guileless. Totally trusting. And just like that, before he could stop it, Nikos felt a sharp pain near his heart, as if it was expanding and cracking apart. For the first time in his life he had the sense that he was utterly insignificant. That this baby was literally the most important thing in the world. And he would do anything to prevent any harm coming to a hair on his head.

Daniel moved then, and Nikos's heart stopped as he instinctively tightened his hold on him. He realised how fragile he was. How easily he could be hurt. And Nikos felt fear.

The tendrils of that disturbing memory snaked around him again. Surely his father had had a moment like this? Holding Nikos in his arms? Feeling the same things? And yet he'd still abandoned his son. As had his mother.

It was as if Daniel could see all the way into his soul, to where Nikos had always felt so hollow. To where he'd been abandoned by his own parents because he hadn't been good enough…lovable enough. How could he give this child something he'd never experienced himself?

Cold sweat pickled over his skin and Nikos handed Daniel back into Maggie's safe arms.

He barely heard her say, 'That was really good…you're a natural…'

He had to get out *now*.

He left the room and went straight to the bathroom and locked himself inside. It took extreme effort and willpower not to be sick. He looked at himself in the mirror, but didn't really notice how wild he looked, his skin pale and clammy.

Eventually the nausea subsided and his chest felt less tight. *Theos.* He couldn't even hold his own baby without almost having a panic attack. And he hadn't had one of those since he'd gone to boarding school, where they'd been beaten out of him by the older boys.

After a few minutes there was a light knock on the door.

'Nikos? Are you okay?'

CHAPTER SEVEN

NIKOS'S HANDS TIGHTENED on the sink. He took a deep breath. The door opened behind him.

'Nikos?'

He lifted his head, saw Maggie reflected behind him in the mirror. Her hair was a vivid splash of red and gold against the white marble of the bathroom. He turned around. He still felt shaky, as if a layer of skin had been peeled away.

Maggie came further in and Nikos wanted to tell her not to come any closer. Because he knew what he needed right now, to eclipse this pervading spread of vulnerability, and it was something only she could give him.

Even that unsettling revelation wasn't enough to jolt him out of this mood, so he said nothing. He let her keep coming. Closer. Like Red Riding Hood approaching the big bad wolf.

She was frowning. 'What *was* that, Nikos? You looked like you'd seen a ghost.'

'Is Daniel okay?' he asked.

She frowned again. 'He's fine. He's already asleep. Nikos, you didn't hurt him.'

He shook his head. 'It wasn't that… I just…'

'What *was* it?'

Nikos put up a hand. 'You shouldn't come any closer.'

Maggie could feel the unmistakable electric charge in the atmosphere. Her body was reacting to it, making her want to move closer to Nikos even though the warned her not to.

She knew she should turn and leave—clearly he didn't want her here—but there was something in his face, in his eyes, that told a different story.

He needed her.

She didn't even know how she knew that—she just did.

She could only guess that holding his baby for the first time had been about as cataclysmic as it had been for her when Daniel had been born.

She tried again. 'What just happened?'

He shook his head. 'I can't explain it… *Theos*, Maggie, just get out.'

Maggie's heart spasmed at the raw tone in Nikos's voice. 'Why?'

'Because if you don't I'll have to touch you.'

Her pulse tripped and started again at a faster rate. 'Why would that be a bad thing?'

Nikos's jaw clenched. 'Because I don't feel very gentle right now.'

His warning didn't scare her—it excited her.

She told him without words that he could touch her if he wanted to by stepping right in front of him.

Nikos said warningly, 'Maggie...' But there was something unguarded in his expression. In his voice.

She lifted a hand and touched his jaw, felt the stubble tickling her palm. He caught her hand and turned it, pressing a kiss to the centre, flicking out his tongue. Her insides seized on a spasm of lust.

When he bent his head she was already reaching up, meeting him halfway. Mouths collided as her arms slid around his neck. She was arching her body even closer. Nothing could hold her back from this.

She was vaguely aware of Nikos lifting her and settling her onto a hard surface. The bathroom counter. It put their mouths on the same level. He tugged at her shirt. She heard something ping. A button? She didn't care. She just wanted Nikos's hands on her bare flesh.

He pushed off her shirt, opened her bra, cupped her breasts. Laved one peak with his tongue and then the other. They were so sensitive... Maggie gripped Nikos's head, her whole body tingling.

His shirt was open—had she done that? She reached for him, pushing it off his wide shoulders. It fell to the ground and she half slipped, half slithered off the counter to reach for his trousers, undoing the belt, then the button, the zip, pulling them down. She was infused with a kind of confidence that would have shocked her if she'd been able to appreciate it.

His erection was long and thick. 'Touch me, Maggie...'

She wrapped her hand around him and he pulsed against her fingers. She moved her hand up and down experimentally and heard Nikos hiss a breath through his teeth.

He reached for her now, opening her jeans, tugging them down, taking her underwear with them. Then he lifted her again, back onto the marble surface. Her hands were dislodged from his erection and they went to his chest, fingers tangling in the dark hair curling over his pectorals.

A very feminine part of her exulted in his virile masculinity. It roused something that felt very primal in her. He pushed her legs apart, coming between them, and at the same time captured her mouth again.

He put his hand on her, between her legs. She could feel how hot she was. How damp. She might have been embarrassed if she hadn't felt so needy. She pushed against him, silently begging him to—

She gasped when he answered her silent plea,

exploring her with his fingers, sinking them deep into her slick body.

But it wasn't enough. She pulled back and reached for Nikos's body again, wrapping her hand around him, drawing him to where she wanted him to fill her, to eclipse all the questions and fears in her head.

'Please, Nikos…'

He took his hand away and put his arm around her back, nudging her legs even further apart. And then, with one powerful thrust, he was there…deep in the heart of her body…where she'd dreamt of him for a whole year.

Pleasure exploded outwards to his every extremity. *This*, Nikos thought as he plunged deep inside Maggie's tight, slick body. *This* was what he needed. Over and over again.

And then she was quivering in his arms, both their bodies slick, their breath coming in short, sharp gasps, as with one final thrust Nikos's thoughts went blank and were replaced with pure ecstasy. The kind of pleasure and transcendence that went above and beyond anything that could be synthetically made by humans. Pleasure in its purest form.

Maggie's body convulsed powerfully around his, causing him to shudder against her as another tide of pleasure swept over him.

* * *

Maggie was barely aware of Nikos extricating himself, helping her off the marble counter, handing her her trousers. Her shirt was open, her bra undone. She felt…turned inside out. The whole thing had been fast and furious, and yet she was suffused with lingering pleasure and a sense of satisfaction that made her want to lie down and sleep for a hundred years.

She could sense the tension in Nikos. When she'd put on her underwear and jeans and pulled her shirt together she looked at him. He was grim-faced. The suspicion that he regretted what had just happened made her feel exposed. She'd all but thrown herself at him…lust overriding every other thought.

'What is it?' Her voice was croaky.

'We didn't use protection.'

Maggie struggled to make her brain work. She wasn't unduly concerned. 'I haven't started my periods again yet… I won't while I'm breastfeeding. It's highly unlikely that we're in danger.'

'I was careless. I won't be next time.'

Because he didn't want children.

Reality slid back like a traitor as she remembered what had precipitated this explosive interlude.

She moved past him to the door. 'I should check on Daniel.'

As she went back out into the apartment she realised the magnitude of what had just happened. They hadn't even been in the apartment for an hour and they'd made love. *Combusted.*

Daniel was still fast asleep. Maggie went onto the terrace, feeling raw. She wasn't in her right mind around Nikos. She couldn't see straight… think straight.

She wasn't sure what she'd hoped for when she'd put Daniel into Nikos's arms—maybe, naively, some kind of idyllic bonding moment, with him weeping tears of emotion as he lifted his baby and proclaimed, *My son!*

She heard a sound behind her and turned around. Nikos was watching her. She felt vulnerable.

'Maggie…that shouldn't have—'

She put up a hand. 'It's okay—you don't have to tell me it shouldn't have happened. I know.'

He frowned and walked towards her. 'I wasn't going to say that. I was going to say it shouldn't have happened *like that*.'

Maggie knew she should let this go. She really didn't want to hear Nikos articulating that he couldn't bond with his son, but she had to know what she was dealing with.

'Why did it happen? What was going on with you?'

For a long moment he said nothing. Then he moved to the wall, putting his hands on it. Maggie turned around to watch him. Nikos didn't look at her.

'I've never held a baby before. He's so small and defenceless. But *strong*. I felt it…'

He turned around, a stark expression on his face.

'I wasn't loved, Maggie. By my parents or my grandparents. Even if my mother *did* love me I was too small to remember what that felt like.'

He shook his head.

'I don't want Daniel to experience what I did, but already I know he won't. Because he has you and you love him. I just can't promise to…to give him something I never experienced myself.'

Maggie took this in and tried to ignore the ache near her heart at the thought of Nikos as a lonely child. 'But I know you felt something powerful just now when you held him. I saw it.'

'I realised how vulnerable he is. And how much I want to protect him.'

Nikos looked tortured. A million miles from the careless charming playboy she'd first met. She wanted to tell him that wanting to protect his son *was* a form of love, but knew it would sound like a platitude.

'Okay,' she said after a moment.

'Okay?'

She made a little shrugging motion. 'That's good enough.'

Was it good enough, though?

Nikos said, 'I'm committed to making this relationship work for the sake of our son.'

Committed. In a way, Maggie couldn't fault Nikos. He was already offering more than her father had ever offered *her*. And she had seen powerful emotion affect him just now, so it was surely only a matter of time before he realised that what he felt for his son *was* love. Even if he didn't think he wasn't capable of it.

To her shame, she felt a dart of something like envy. For her own son. Because he'd sparked something in Nikos that would flower to life. It couldn't *not*. But as for her...? Why was she even thinking of herself in this equation? She didn't even—

Her thoughts stopped there.

The problem was that she *did* have feelings for him. She'd had them since that night a year ago, when his note the next day had been like a punch to the gut. And then each day of a whole year had followed and he hadn't made contact— a further punch to the gut. Even knowing now that it hadn't been his fault, because he'd never got the note, it didn't diminish the hurt. Because he wouldn't have contacted her anyway.

Maggie knew she needed to cut off all these nascent tender feelings she had for Nikos, because he'd told her more than once that he just wasn't capable of returning them. He never would have offered her a relationship if it hadn't been for Daniel. The fact that he might come to love his son would have to be enough for her.

She said, 'I'm committed too.' But the words tasted tart on her tongue.

Nikos moved closer and sneaked a hand around the back of her neck. Her traitorous heart leapt, along with her pulse.

'I think we have a lot going for us, Maggie. I like you, and I want to be a good father for Daniel. We have insane chemistry. We want each other. We're going into this with eyes wide open—no illusions. That's as good a foundation for marriage as any I know.'

I like you.

Maggie longed to be able to pull back and tell Nikos that liking wasn't good enough. But this wasn't about her. And she was afraid that he would touch her again and see how close to the surface her emotions were.

She reached for his hand and pulled it down. 'I think I'll go and get Daniel settled in our new rooms.'

Nikos looked at her as if he was trying to figure her out. Then he took a step back. He glanced at his watch. 'I should go to the office to catch up on some work and clear my schedule before the wedding. Help yourself to dinner and make a list of things you need for Daniel. I'll make sure you get everything you need.'

Maggie watched Nikos walk out and exhaled

once she was alone again. Her body was still over-sensitised and her heart was still bruised. As if on cue, to remind her of what was at stake here, Daniel made a sound, and she went in to find him awake. He regarded her with those steady dark eyes. Dark eyes with hazel flecks…

She pushed everything else out of her mind and tended to her son, telling herself that she and Daniel had a lot to be thankful for. Nikos might have proved to be just like her father, uncaring and uninterested. The fact that he wasn't should be a relief. To want anything more—like love and a real family—was just being greedy.

The next day Maggie stood in front of a full-length mirror, but the woman reflected back at her was a stranger. It was her—but not her. She was tall and svelte, with sleek wavy hair twisted up into an elegant chignon. She'd never thought her hair could behave like that, but the hairdresser in the hotel salon had cultivated it into something far less wild.

And she'd had a pedicure and manicure.

But the dress…

Maggie had never worn a long dress before. Not even for her end-of-school dance. Because she hadn't gone as she'd had no date. None of the boys had wanted to ask 'Beanpole Maggie' as they'd have looked small next to her.

The dress was black and off the shoulder, with

little dropped sleeves that rested on her arms. Maggie had tried pulling them up but the stylist had said, '*Non, non, cherie*—they're meant to be like that.'

A sweetheart neckline showed more skin than Maggie had ever shown before. The tops of her breasts swelled against the bodice in a way that felt indecent. The material clung to her breasts, her belly, waist and hips, before falling to the floor in a swathe of material. When she moved a slit up one side revealed her leg.

She felt very pale, and wished she had more colour.

There was a movement behind her and she saw Nikos, reflected in the doorway.

Her heart stopped. He was wearing a tuxedo and she felt a rushing sensation in her head, remembering the first time she'd seen him lounging against his own front door, looking like the devil himself.

He looked no less innocent now, even though his tuxedo was pristine. He oozed sophistication and masculine elegance, yet with that ever-present edginess that hinted at something much darker and more intense.

He came into the room and she couldn't take her eyes off him.

His dark gaze swept her up and down. 'I knew you were beautiful, Maggie…but like this you are even more than I imagined.'

Maggie couldn't even take in what he was saying. It was so far removed from her reality.

Her old reality.

'You look…lovely.' She winced inwardly. What did one say to one of the most ridiculously handsome men on the planet?

Nikos quirked a smile. 'Thank you.'

She wanted to scowl. 'You know what I mean… I'm not used to this.'

Nikos's smile faded. He reached out and touched Maggie's jaw. 'I know. You'll be fine. I promise. Everyone will be captivated by you.'

'I don't want to captivate anyone.'

Don't you? whispered a small voice.

She ignored it.

Nikos took his hand away and moved behind her to the boxes laid out on a table. Maggie hadn't even noticed them before.

He opened one of them up and stood back. 'What would you like to wear with the dress?'

Maggie walked over and was almost blinded by the bling. Diamonds… A necklace with square rough-cut diamonds and matching earrings. A bracelet.

She looked at Nikos. 'My ears aren't pierced.'

He responded smoothly. 'Okay, the bracelet and necklace, then.'

He plucked them out and moved behind her to put on the necklace. She felt its heavy cold weight against her collarbone and touched it.

Then he came in front of her and lifted her arm, fastening the bracelet around her wrist. It too was heavy. Substantial.

'What if I lose them?' she asked.

Nikos looked at her. 'Don't. They're worth the annual debt of a small country.'

There was a glimmer of humour in his eyes, though. And then he picked up another, much smaller box.

Maggie looked down at it. 'What's this?'

'This evening is primarily focused on introducing you as my fiancée. You'll need a ring.'

He opened the box and Maggie sucked in a breath. She'd never really been interested in jewellery, but the ring nestled against a white satin cushion was exquisite. It was a square-cut emerald, with small square diamonds on either side, in a platinum setting and band.

Maggie said, 'It's beautiful.'

'I could have let you choose, but I thought this one would suit.'

Nikos took it out of the box and reached for her left hand. She held it out and he slipped the ring onto her ring finger. It fitted.

She looked up. 'How did you know it would fit?'

He let her hand go. 'A lucky guess.'

A little shiver went down Maggie's spine. This was all falling into place so easily.

Nikos stepped back. 'Ready?'

Maggie nodded, but was suddenly reluctant.

Nikos noticed. 'What is it?' he asked.

She bit her lip. 'Daniel... I hope he'll be okay.' She'd left him before, for brief amounts of time, but this was a whole new milieu.

'You like Marianne, don't you?'

She nodded. In the end none of the nannies who'd come for interview had been suitable, and then Mathilde the housekeeper had suggested her twin sister—newly retired from being a schoolteacher and already bored. They'd met, and Maggie had liked her immediately, warming to her easy maternal warmth. And Daniel had liked her too.

'We'll only be gone for a few hours. Mathilde is staying here with Marianne to help her out. And you've expressed milk, haven't you?'

Maggie wasn't unaware of the irony that Nikos was speaking those words out loud: *you've expressed milk*. A far cry from the lexicon of his previous experience.

'Yes.'

'Then let's go. The sooner we go, the sooner we're back.'

Maggie put her head around the door of the kitchen area, where Marianne had Daniel in her arms, making faces at him. He was gurgling and kicking his legs. She caught Maggie's eye and made a shooing motion. Maggie forced a smile, even though she felt physical pain at the thought of leaving Daniel behind.

In the lift on the way down Nikos said, 'It'll get easier. He'll be fine.'

Maggie suddenly felt at odds...out of her depth. Tetchy. 'And you know this because suddenly you're an expert in babies?'

He cast her a look. 'I might have more experience if I'd had more notice.'

Maggie clamped her mouth shut. She felt immediately contrite. 'Sorry. That wasn't fair. It's just hard to leave him behind. What if he—?'

Nikos took her hand, surprising her.

'Then Mathilde or Marianne will call and we'll come back straight away.'

He kept hold of her hand until they were outside, where a sleek car was waiting.

The air was warm and the sky was turning dusky, imbuing the surrounding buildings with a magical light. Maggie got into the back of the car on one side, Nikos the other. The interior was cream leather, sumptuous. When the doors were closed and they moved into the traffic the noises outside were just a dim hum. It was like a luxurious cocoon.

Maggie looked out of the window, taking in the wide elegant streets. They were crossing the Seine. She noticed something in her peripheral vision and looked to see Nikos's fingers drumming a staccato beat on his thigh.

Without thinking, she reached across and put her hand over his.

* * *

Nikos couldn't move his fingers. He looked down to see a pale hand over his, stopping his fingers drumming in that beat that he always felt gave him away.

Maggie's hand was cool on his. She took it away. He looked at her. She was pink.

'Sorry, I don't know why I did that.'

Nikos was more disturbed by her noticing his nervous tic and wanting to soothe it than he cared to admit. He covered it up by drawling, 'Feel free to touch me whenever you want.'

She grew pinker.

Nikos wanted to shake his head. How had he, of all people, ended up with a woman like Maggie? Innocent, gauche. But surprising.

She surprised him now.

'Do you not enjoy social occasions?' she asked.

For the first time in his life Nikos was aware of a sense of reluctance about walking into a room full of people and...*performing*. Because that was what he'd been doing all his life. Performing to try and make his grandparents love him. Rebelling to make his father notice him. Charming and smiling and seducing his way through endless parties, functions and events and women, to perpetuate the myth of being a playboy while taking advantage of anyone who underestimated him.

He was inclined to give Maggie some pithy response, but he surprised himself by saying,

'Would you believe me if I said not as much as people might think?'

Maggie regarded him and shook her head slowly. 'No, I believe you. Why do you do it, then?'

Nikos shrugged, feeling the need to escape Maggie's piercing blue gaze. Was it more piercing this evening? Because of the artful make-up that had elevated her from beautiful to breathtaking?

'It's expected of me. It's an integral part of the world I grew up in and the business we have only enhances that.'

'You'd really have me believe that all these countless premieres and parties where you're photographed with beautiful women are pure torture for you, then?'

Nikos suspected that Maggie had intended that to sound lighter than it had. She looked self-conscious. It reminded him that she was different.

He took her hand and laced her fingers with his, feeling the inevitable tug of desire. 'They're not torture, no. It would be disingenuous to claim that. But those women were passing fancies. Diversions.'

He saw her expression change as his meaning sank in. They might be announcing their engagement tonight, but he still wasn't in the market for anything deep and meaningful.

She pulled her hand from his and looked away—and then she tensed. 'Oh, my God—is that where we're going?'

Nikos looked out of the window to see a hotel entrance lit up like Mardi Gras by the popping flashbulbs of photographers, which were almost out-dazzling the shimmering dresses and jewels of the guests being disgorged onto the red carpet.

'Yes, that's it.'

He looked at Maggie again and saw she was deathly pale.

He took her hand. 'Maggie, look at me.'

She tore her gaze from the scene they were fast approaching. 'I don't think I can do this.'

'Just hold my hand and smile. We're going to stop for a couple of pictures. All you have to do is smile, okay?'

For the first time Nikos felt a prickle of unease. He hadn't really considered what jumping into the deep end would be like for Maggie. Now he felt protective, and it was disconcerting.

Maggie nodded. She looked terrified.

He said, 'Relax. It'll be fine. I promise.'

The car stopped and the door was opened by an usher.

Nikos said, 'Wait there. I'll help you out.'

Maggie's heart was palpitating so hard she felt light-headed. She hadn't really considered the enormity of what this would be like. She'd had some notion that they'd walk anonymously into a function room. Not be paraded in front of the world's media.

Nikos was waiting, holding out a hand. Reluctantly she reached for it and let him help her out. The dress fell around her legs and she walked carefully in the high heels, not used to them, clinging to Nikos's arm to stay upright as much as to disguise her trembling limbs.

They were approaching the entrance now, lined on either side by photographers. Then they stepped onto the red carpet and the world exploded into blinding light.

'Nikos! Nikos!'

Maggie was in shock, clinging on to Nikos as voices came at her from all sides. She couldn't understand French, which was probably a good thing. She felt like Alice in Wonderland—as if she'd landed in a new and scary universe.

Nikos's arm was around her waist, pulling her close. It was enough to distract her momentarily, and then he said in her ear, 'Good… Now just smile and pretend this is normal. Let them see the ring.'

Maggie placed her hand as strategically as she could over Nikos's arm and the flashbulbs increased in intensity. So much so that she felt blinded.

After what felt like an eternity Nikos was saying something back to the photographers and leading her into a thronged foyer which was mercifully absent of flashbulbs. Her ears were ringing.

'Okay?'

She nodded, even though she felt stunned. Dizzy.

Waiters dressed in black were handing out tall, slim glasses of champagne. Nikos handed her one. She took a sip, aware that she shouldn't really drink too much, but she relished the alcohol fizzing down into her belly and sending out a little warming, calming glow.

Nikos looked as if he was about to say something else, but then they were joined by a tall man—as tall and dark as Nikos. Intimidatingly good-looking with deep-set dark eyes. He also looked slightly familiar, which was odd when Maggie knew he was a stranger. He had a forbidding expression.

Maggie sensed Nikos's tension. Then, 'Maggie, I'd like to introduce you to Sharif, my brother.'

So that was why he was familiar-looking. Maggie could see the resemblance now. The same high cheekbones. Strong bone structure. Thick hair. Arrogant air.

He put out a hand. 'It is a pleasure to make your acquaintance, Maggie. And I believe congrautlations are in order? On your forthcoming marriage and also because you've made me an uncle?'

For the first time Maggie had a very real sense that she and Daniel had joined a family.

She shook Sharif's hand, more than a little intimidated. 'Yes, thank you. His name is Daniel. He's three months old.'

Sharif let her hand go and slid a look to his brother. 'I look forward to meeting him soon. Perhaps at your wedding?'

Maggie nodded. 'Of course. He'll be there.'

Sharif addressed Nikos. 'So, are you still okay to do the tour or do I need to talk to Maks?'

Nikos answered. 'It's fine. We'll have a brief honeymoon and then I'll resume my work commitments.'

Sharif gave Nikos a nod, then made his excuses and walked away.

Maggie turned to Nikos. 'What was he talking about…the tour? And a brief honeymoon? Why do we need any honeymoon?'

Nikos said, 'We need a honeymoon to make our marriage look authentic, so we're going to spend a couple of days in Athens. The tour he spoke of is a showcasing of various aspects of the Marchetti Group in Rome, Madrid, London, France and Monte Carlo—from the launch of a new perfume to welcoming a new head designer for one of our fashion houses and hosting various charity benefits. It'll be a quick, fast-paced tour, over two weeks. We're building up our exposure for the thirtieth anniversary of the group next year.'

Maggie arched a brow. 'And was any of this going to be discussed with *me*? I know this marriage is just for show, and for Daniel's sake, but I do deserve to know what's happening.'

To her surprise, Nikos said, 'Yes, you're right, and I'm sorry. I'm not used to having to explain my schedule to anyone else.'

She was a little mollified by his response.

And then he asked, 'Do you think it's feasible for us to do the tour with Daniel?'

Maggie shrugged lightly. 'If we have Marianne with us it should be okay. He's portable at the moment. Obviously as he gets older things will be much trickier. We'll have to have more of a base.'

Maggie felt a pang as she said that. Nikos's apartment wasn't exactly the kind of home she'd envisaged. But maybe she needed to be more accepting of this new life and give it a chance.

After that they were sucked into a round of greeting people. Maggie was aware of lots of stares and whispers and did her best to ignore them. At first she tried to remember names and faces, but it soon became impossible so she gave up.

She noticed that Nikos had an assistant on hand, to help jog his memory with a name in case he forgot. What hope did she have?

'Ready to go?' asked Nikos.

Maggie looked at him, feeling guilty. Had he noticed her moving from one foot to the other to relieve the ache in the balls of her feet? Had she looked as bored as she'd felt over the past couple of hours?

'Can we?' she asked.

He nodded, then took her hand to lead her through the crowd. When he stopped suddenly she collided with his back.

He turned around. 'You did really well this evening.'

Maggie looked up at him, feeling a ridiculous flush of pleasure warming her insides. 'Really?'

He nodded and, to her surprise, reached out and tucked a wayward lock of hair behind one ear. His hand lingered and then caught behind her head. Before she could prepare herself his mouth was covering hers in a searing brand of heat.

Maggie swayed towards him, the kiss making her feel more drunk than the half-glass of champagne she'd had at the start of the evening.

When he pulled back she looked up. 'What was that for?' He didn't strike her as the sort of guy to indulge in a PDA.

'There's a photographer over there. I thought it would be good to give him something.'

The flush of heat in Maggie's body drained away. He'd kissed her for a photographer. Not because he hadn't been able to help himself. Of *course* a man like him wouldn't indulge in PDAs.

Maggie tugged herself free. 'I need to get back to Daniel.'

She walked towards the entrance.

Nikos watched her go for a second. It had been harder than he'd expected or appreciated to pull back from that kiss just now. It might have started as something strategic, but it had become something else as soon as their mouths had touched.

She cut an effortlessly graceful figure now, walking through the crowd with a sensuality Nikos felt she wasn't even aware of. Who could have known that such a swan had been hidden under that casual appearance?

For a man who would usually abhor kissing a woman in public—even a lover—it had been surprisingly easy to turn to Maggie and kiss her. Not just because of the opportunity presented but because he'd needed to after an evening of her surprisingly easy presence by his side.

The crowd was closing in behind Maggie and she'd disappeared from view. Nikos moved to catch up, not liking the way he couldn't see her bright hair. He was almost at the entrance before he saw her again, and the feeling of relief that went through him was uncomfortable.

What was wrong with him? She wasn't going anywhere. She was his. Daniel was his. And he *would* make this work.

They were almost back at the hotel when Nikos asked, 'What is it, Maggie? You've barely said a word since we left.'

She was still angry—*hurt* by the calculated kiss. 'I don't appreciate being used as a PR stunt.

If you're going to do that again then please tell me in advance.'

When she glanced at him she saw he looked blank.

'The kiss?' she prompted.

Comprehension dawned. 'You thought I just kissed you for that?'

'That's what you said.'

'I took advantage of an opportunity that presented itself—but, believe me, I didn't kiss you just for that.'

'What does *that* mean?'

'It means that right now there's nothing strategic to be gained but still I want to kiss you.'

'Oh.'

'But this isn't the right place.'

Maggie's heart palpitated. 'No.'

He took her hand and lifted it up. His warm breath feathered across her palm. She shivered with awareness. He pressed his mouth there, his tongue flicking out to touch her skin, inducing another shiver.

As the car stopped outside the hotel he said in a low voice, 'That kiss might have started out as a strategic thing, but it didn't end up as one. I never do anything I don't want to, Maggie.'

He let her go then, and got out of the car.

She didn't even look at him the whole way up to the apartment in the lift. She went straight to her bedroom, firmly closing the door behind her. She rested against it for a moment before she went to check on Daniel, her pulse racing, skin prickling all over.

Damn Nikos. She would have to be so careful around him or he would incinerate her.

CHAPTER EIGHT

THE DAY OF the wedding a week later was warm and sultry. Maggie and Nikos were travelling together to the civil register office. Daniel was in the car behind them with Marianne.

Nothing so romantic as her groom waiting at the top of an aisle to greet her. She was surprised at the pang of regret she felt that she wouldn't get to have that experience of watching someone she loved turn to greet her as she walked towards them.

It irritated her that the only person she could envisage in that scenario had all too familiar dark and devilishly handsome features. Thick curling hair…

'Why are you scowling?'

Maggie looked at Nikos. She'd barely seen him since the other night. He'd been working until late each evening—which Maggie had appreciated but also felt conflicted by, not liking the way she'd noticed his absence so keenly.

But she'd been busy herself—settling in with

Daniel. Making sure she had all she needed for him. Doing up his room. Going through the clothes that the stylist had stocked her walk-in wardrobe with, feeling totally intimidated by all the silk and chiffon and elegant trouser suits. Chatting with Mathilde and Marianne, who were becoming good friends.

Mathilde had confided in Maggie that she was glad to see Nikos settle down, because she'd always felt he cut such a lonely figure. Maggie had smiled and said nothing, knowing that Nikos would bristle at the idea that anyone thought he was lonely.

Nikos was looking at her. She rearranged her features into a smile.

'That's marginally better. Aren't you delighted to be marrying the man of your dreams today?'

She could handle this charming Nikos, who mocked her. It reminded her of the man who had seduced her so easily.

Maggie affected a look of surprise. 'Oh? The man of my dreams is here? Where is he?'

She pretended to look around and Nikos emitted a short laugh. 'Don't tell me you're still holding a torch for Mr Nice and Boring?'

'It's a bit late for regrets now—and someone once told me regrets were for losers,' Maggie said lightly even though she wondered if Nikos was a mind-reader.

'That someone must have been very intelligent.'

Maggie was sorry for goading him now. It only reminded her of his note, and the fact that she wouldn't be here if it wasn't for Daniel.

The car was pulling to a stop in a square now. Maggie suddenly felt nervous. Nikos took her hand. She looked at him.

'You look beautiful. And, for what it's worth, I hadn't ever expected to be in this situation, but I'm glad it's with you.'

Maggie couldn't tear her gaze away from Nikos's. She couldn't fault him for leading her on with false hope and promises. He'd been very clear they were doing this for Daniel.

'Ready?'

Maggie nodded and tried to swallow her nerves.

She waited till the driver had opened her door and Nikos was waiting to help her out. She was wearing a fitted white blazer over a very simple but elegant white silk dress, cut on the bias. It fell to just below her knees and she wore satin kitten-heel shoes.

Her hair was up and she wore a small hat with a piece of net that came down over her eyes. Clip-on pearls in her ears and her engagement ring were her only jewellery.

Marianne got out of the car behind them and Maggie went over to make sure Daniel was okay. He looked adorable, in a romper suit in a royal blue that matched the same blue in Nikos's three-piece suit.

She knew she couldn't delay any longer, so she shot Marianne a smile—the nanny smiled back reassuringly—and went over to Nikos, who took her hand to lead her into the office.

Maggie was surprised to see more than a few people there. She recognised Sharif, and there was another tall man, very lean, with short dark blond hair. Spectacularly gorgeous. He had to be Maks. Beside him was a young woman.

Maggie was too nervous to dwell on who everyone else was and tried to focus on the ceremony, led by a registrar who conducted it in English for her benefit. She made a mental note to learn French as soon as possible. After all, Daniel was a quarter Greek and Italian and would be growing up in France. A true child of Europe.

'You may now kiss your bride.'

Maggie panicked. It was over already?

She turned to face Nikos. He tipped up her chin with a finger and pulled her close. She cursed him for putting on a show.

He smiled. 'No regrets, Mrs Marchetti.'

Before she could say anything he was kissing her, and her brain fused with heat. She hadn't built all the sophisticated defences she'd need around Nikos yet. She probably never would.

When they walked out of the office some minutes later Nikos warned her, 'There'll be a few photographers. Not a crowd like the other night, though.'

Sure enough there were a handful, and they stopped and posed for pictures. One of them called out, '*Baisez!*' and Maggie soon figured out what that meant when Nikos pulled her close for another kiss.

By the time they got to one of the most exclusive Marchetti hotels in the centre of Paris for the wedding breakfast Maggie's whole body was one big mass of quivering nerve-endings and overload of adrenalin.

'So you're Maggie?'

Maggie turned around, a smile fixed on her face. It was the blond man she'd noticed standing near Sharif in the register office.

She held out her hand. 'Yes—you must be Maks?'

'Guilty.' He shook her hand. He was very different from both Nikos and Sharif, and yet similar. More guarded. Intense grey eyes.

'I'd say welcome to the family,' he drawled. 'But that would imply that we're some kind of functioning unit.'

He looked over Maggie's head and she followed his gaze.

'That's my younger sister, Sasha.'

Maggie took in the woman she'd thought might be his girlfriend. She was beautiful in a way that made Maggie suspect she tried to hide it. She was dressed almost frumpily, in a long skirt and a high-necked blouse, but she recognised the bone structure. Maggie felt an affinity with the girl, even though they hadn't yet met. She recognised something about the way she was trying to hide herself.

'You look alike,' she said.

'We take after our mother. Nikos and Sharif bear the brunt of the Marchetti genes. Sasha has a different father from me and my brothers. She made a lucky escape in that regard.'

Maggie was just absorbing this, and how complicated this family was, when she heard a voice.

'Filling my wife's head with nonsense, Maks?'

She felt a jolt at the words *'my wife'*. Nikos slid an arm around her waist.

Maks smiled, but it didn't reach his eyes. 'Not at all, I was merely welcoming Maggie to the firm.'

Nikos made a sound that might have been a laugh or a snarl. 'If you don't mind, I need to steal my wife away. We're leaving for our honeymoon.'

Maks inclined his head. *'Bon voyage* and best wishes to you both.'

Nikos made efficient work of saying goodbye to everyone, and soon he was leading Maggie out of the hotel and into a waiting car. He undid his tie. Marianne had gone ahead with Daniel to the private plane, taking Maggie's expressed milk with her to feed the baby. They were going to

Athens for a couple of days—ostensibly for their honeymoon, but also so that Nikos could check in on his Athens office.

There was a brooding energy surrounding him that she tried to dissipate by saying, 'Maks told me about Sasha...that she's not your sister.'

Nikos glanced at her and then away. 'I never spent any time with her growing up in any case—she made a lucky escape.'

'That's what he said too—or something like it. Was your father really so bad?'

Nikos made a slightly strangled sound. 'Yes. The only thing he did for us was to create a legacy that we must nurture and grow.'

'So what's Maks's role in the business?'

'He's involved in the fashion and branding end of things.'

'It's a pity you and your half-brothers aren't closer. It was just me and my mum. I always wished I had siblings. I don't even have cousins.'

She was about to add that she'd always intended having more than one child, but clamped her mouth shut.

Nikos usually resented any intrusion into his personal life, but Maggie was now his wife. He also didn't like being reminded of when he'd been younger, when he'd wished that he and his brothers were closer.

But reluctantly he confided, 'It was as if our

father deliberately did all he could to keep us apart. Probably to keep us from uniting against him. I think he was afraid that we might do a better job than him, and while he wanted us to succeed him, he only handed over full control through his death.'

He looked at Maggie. 'What's your impression of my brothers?'

'Maks is intense. Sharif is impenetrable.'

'And me?'

Maggie went a bit pink. 'Charming—but you're hiding something much more serious. That evening you arrived at Kildare House, on first appearance I thought you were drunk. But you weren't drunk at all.'

Nikos was surprised at her assessment.

She saw too much.

He needed to deflect her attention from him now.

'The one thing me and my brothers have in common is that our father let all of us down.'

'That's sad.'

Nikos shrugged. 'Is it? Maybe it's better to find out early who you can depend on in life.'

Hours later, Maggie still felt an ache near her heart to think of Nikos and his half-brothers growing up separated by an insecure and domineering father. They'd arrived a short time before at the penthouse apartment of the most exclusive hotel in Athens—one of the Marchetti Group's jewels.

A grand classic building, it stood on one of Athens' oldest squares, and from its penthouse they had unimpeded views of the hilly city of Athens and the Acropolis.

Marianne was walking around with Daniel, oohing and ahing at the view. Nikos was due to take Maggie out for dinner and she'd just expressed some more milk for Daniel.

She'd changed out of her wedding outfit and into a pair of long trousers and a matching long-sleeved silk top with a round neck. Simple, but elegant. Her stylist had called ahead to the boutique at the hotel and ensured that Maggie's wardrobe there would be stocked with suitable clothes.

Now she had taken her hair down and was massaging her skull, which was sore from all the pins holding her hair up.

'Sorry, I had to take a call.'

She turned around to see Nikos walk in, adjusting his jacket. He'd changed too, into a steel-grey suit, and he looked so vital and handsome that her breath caught. He looked up, and that gaze raked her up and down. A flash of heat sizzled straight to her core.

He said, 'You look beautiful.'

Maggie was embarrassed. She wasn't used to compliments. She wasn't sure she'd ever get used to them. 'Thank you.'

'Ready?'

'Will there be paparazzi?'

'Most likely.'

Maggie swallowed her trepidation. She'd jumped into the deep end with this man a year ago, had his baby three months ago, and married him today. She could handle some photographers. She'd get used to it.

She'd have to.

'Would you like to go dancing?'

Maggie looked at Nikos across the table. *'Dancing?'*

He sat forward. 'Yes—you know… Somewhere they play loud music and people move energetically in a communal space.'

Maggie made a face, but her pulse was racing. This evening…this restaurant…had been the kind of date she'd never dreamed of, because it would have been way beyond her fantasies.

The restaurant Nikos had taken her to was high in a glass building with views of the Acropolis lit up at night. The lighting was golden and everyone in the place looked impossibly charismatic, beautiful. Gilded.

People had stopped and stared as Nikos and she had entered. She'd stumbled a little on the way to their table. But Nikos had put a hand to her back to steady her.

The food had been exquisite morsels of the

freshest ingredients Maggie had ever tasted. She'd longed to go to the kitchen and talk to the chefs.

During dinner, Nikos had said to her, 'It's refreshing to be with someone who actually likes food.'

Maggie had looked up, her mouth full. When she'd been able to speak she'd said dryly, 'I'll take that as a compliment, shall I?'

She was in danger of being seduced all over again on another level. She put down her napkin now and looked at him suspiciously. 'Why do you want to take me dancing?'

A look passed across his face so fast she couldn't decipher it. Then he leant back and said, 'Full disclosure? For two reasons. One, because I would like to dance with you, and two, we will be seen—and that's a good thing to keep the gossip websites happy.'

Something deflated inside Maggie. Of course. She kept forgetting that everything was really an opportunity to be seen. Most likely even coming to this restaurant.

She shrugged as if she didn't really care. 'Okay, sure.'

As they walked out Nikos was aware of the fact that that had probably been the least enthusiastic response he'd ever got from a woman, and that not only was he drawing looks on the way out, so was Maggie.

And who could blame them? She stood out, with her height, her pale colouring and russet golden hair. Like a magnificent Valkyrie.

Nikos couldn't even recall the type of woman he'd wanted before. They had literally paled into insignificance in his memory.

He only wanted *this* woman.

But he'd never wanted another woman exclusively beyond for a night or two. Uneasiness prickled over his skin and he dismissed it. Whatever this was with Maggie, surely it was a *good* thing that he wanted his wife? He wanted to make this relationship work. He wanted to be a good father to his son.

The thought of anything deeper…he didn't know if he was capable of that.

Maggie wasn't sure where the pounding of her blood stopped and the pounding of the bass began. The beat was moving through her and it was infectious.

They'd taken a short journey to this club, where Nikos had been waved in like royalty. It was a big, cavernous space, with VIP areas around the edge of the first floor, from where they could look down on the dance floor filled with people dancing sinuously.

Maggie was fascinated, sipping her mocktail.

Then Nikos stood up, holding out a hand. 'Come on.'

Maggie put down her drink. 'Down there?' Her voice squeaked, which thankfully he wouldn't notice over the music.

He nodded.

Reluctantly Maggie took Nikos's hand and let him lead her down. As they got to the dance floor the beat changed to something much sultrier and slower. Maggie wasn't sure whether to be relieved or not. She'd dreaded looking like a fool—but now, when Nikos pulled her close, she dreaded him seeing how much of an effect he had on her.

He placed his hands on her hips, bringing her in close to where she could feel every part of his whipcord body, and as they started to move she felt the evidence of his desire.

Naturally her arms went around his neck, bringing them into closer contact. Heat and need suffused every cell in Maggie's body. Surely this had to be the definition of dirty dancing? She tipped her head back to look at Nikos. His eyes were glittering...his jaw was tight.

She wasn't aware of the hundreds of other people around them. It was as if they were in a bubble. He bent his head and after an infinitesimal moment, covered her mouth with his.

The music seemed to be pounding in time with her heart.

Nikos's hands smoothed down her back, the slippery material of her shirt making her skin tingle all over. His arousal pressed against her and Maggie thought she might melt into a puddle right there.

Then she remembered where she was, and with whom. She pulled back, dizzy. 'Is this for show?'

He shook his head. 'No. It's because I want you. Let's get out of here.'

Maggie was about to say, *But we just got here!* but Nikos was leading her back upstairs, picking up their things and leading her outside.

The cool air was like a slap to her face. Waking her up. Nikos's hand was still tight on hers. It was truly shocking how easily he affected her, spinning her out of all control.

His car appeared and he opened the door for her, letting her go. By the time he got into the other side she felt marginally composed again. Composed enough to realise just how much had happened in one day. They were *married*. And this man was still such an enigma to her.

When they got back to the apartment Nikos turned to face her, stark intent on his face. 'Maggie, I want you.'

It was the hardest thing in the world to resist the effect of those words, coming from that man, with *that* look on his face, He was overwhelming. But she had to resist. She needed space to absorb everything or she'd lose herself entirely.

She shook her head. 'I'm quite tired. I'm going to bed.'

He came close. 'This is our wedding night,

agapi mou, and I want my wife. Believe me, the irony of being married and wanting my wife is not something I ever expected to experience.'

If he could have said anything to firm her resolve it was that. This wasn't a real wedding night and she suddenly realised that she wanted it to be. And if he touched her now he would see just how much her emotions were affected.

She stepped back. 'It's been a long day.'

Nikos's mouth thinned. 'I don't play games, Maggie.'

'I'm not playing games. I wouldn't know how.' *Believe me.*

Nikos reached out a finger and trailed it over her jaw. Maggie felt her nipples tighten into buds of need. She gritted her jaw.

Nikos said, 'Oh, I don't doubt for a second that you'd become as proficient as any other woman, given the right circumstances.'

Maggie jerked her head away. 'Don't you ever get tired of being so cynical and suspicious?' She was *glad* she was resisting him now.

Nikos let out a tortured-sounding laugh. 'Believe me, I used to be a lot worse. You're doing something to me. Addling my brain. You've enslaved me, Maggie—does that make you happy? I haven't been able to look at another woman since I met you.'

Nikos's words took a moment to impact on her,

and when they did she said faintly, 'I didn't think you meant that.'

His face was stark with need. 'I told you, Maggie. You haunted me for a year. You ruined me for any other woman. I only want *you.*'

Maggie's heart stopped and then started again. She looked at him. He wasn't lying. Why would he? Surely if he wanted to boost his pride he'd claim she'd been only one of many?

'Wow…'

He arched a brow, his mouth turned up wryly. 'Wow?'

Then, to Maggie's surprise, he took a step back.

He said, 'I won't ever make you do something you don't want to do, Maggie. But we are married and we want each other—a bonus in this marriage. Like I said, I don't play games.'

He turned and walked away from her. She had to clamp her mouth shut in case she called out and told him she'd changed her mind. Then he really would think she was playing games. And she needed this respite.

Nikos's words reverberated in her head. He was a proud man—she knew that. And yet he'd just told her that she'd ruined him for all other women.

Before she did something stupid she went into her room. Checked on Daniel—the reason for this whole union even if Nikos *did* want her. And she wanted him…

It took her hours to fall asleep that night. And the revelation that he hadn't slept with anyone since her hit her anew when she woke in the morning. She knew it really shouldn't mean anything, but she couldn't help her silly heart beating a little too fast every time she thought about it.

She knew it was dangerous to contemplate, but the fact that he wanted her and she wanted him… Surely it went beyond the purely physical? Or could?

But Maggie grimaced. He still hadn't really bonded with Daniel. If he couldn't bond with his baby then what chance did *she* have?

When Maggie emerged into the breakfast room with Daniel, Nikos wasn't there. But there was a note and a mobile phone.

Your new phone. I've sent you a text. N.

She picked up the phone and read the text.

We're going to a party tonight. Need to be ready to leave at six p.m. Is this okay?

Maggie figured that at least he was *asking* her. Not ordering her.

She typed back a quick text.

Yes, fine. X

Then she quickly deleted the X and sent it.

'You didn't say we were leaving Athens to go to the party,' Maggie commented drily as she preceded Nikos back into the apartment later that night.

Her insides were still swooping after their return journey in the small sleek helicopter that had taken them to the island and back.

To her surprise it had been an enjoyable evening, an informal event celebrating the eightieth birthday of an old friend of Nikos's grandparents. Alexiou Spinakis.

The small, rocky and idyllic island had been covered in wild flowers and was full of exotic scents. They'd arrived as the sun was setting, and it had been the most magical sight Maggie had ever seen. And then they'd returned to see Athens lit up underneath them like a glittering carpet of jewels.

She slipped off her heels, giving a small groan of relief. She turned to face Nikos, whose shirt was open, his jacket off and slung over his shoulder, held by one finger. He looked thoroughly disreputable, and Maggie's body tingled all over after an evening spent in such close proximity with him.

In a bid to defuse the ever-simmering physical

awareness, Maggie said, 'I really liked Alexiou. He was sweet.'

Nikos smiled. 'He liked you—the old goat.'

Maggie made a face. 'It wasn't like that. He really loves you, you know. And I can see that you care for him.'

Nikos's face became impassive. 'He was kind to me.'

'It's more than that—he considers you family.'

Maggie felt vulnerable all of a sudden, when she realised that she'd seen a totally different side to Nikos that evening. He'd been at home in his environment, relaxed in a way she'd never seen before. And clearly, he cared for the older man who'd evidently been more of a grandparent to Nikos than his own blood family.

With each layer stripped away he was revealing more of the complex man underneath, and she felt she had to protect herself more.

Terrified that he might touch her, or see even a hint of the vulnerability she felt, she stepped back and said, 'I should go and let Marianne know we're back. I told her not to worry about the night feeds tonight.'

Maggie turned and walked away and Nikos had to battle with himself not to beg her to stop and stay. Her words *he considers you family* reverberated in his head. He didn't need family. But the truth was that Maggie was his family now.

And Daniel. No matter how alien it felt. No matter how terrifying.

He watched the green silk of her dress billowing around her body. She'd taken her shoes off and carried them in one hand. Her hair was loose and wild. That dress had been driving him crazy all night, making his hands itch to slide underneath it and cup her breasts.

He wanted nothing more than to go after her and sink deep inside her, where he didn't have to think. Or feel. But their son needed her.

For the first time in Nikos's life he had to acknowledge the novel sensation of someone else taking precedence over him. He also had to acknowledge that, as much as he wanted Maggie, he didn't relish those far too incisive blue eyes searching his soul for why he always felt such a mix of emotions when he saw his old friend, Alexiou.

He'd always been there for Nikos in a way his family never had. Alexiou used to visit him at boarding school, whenever he'd been in England on business. Even though Nikos had been an angry, surly youth.

The older man would ruffle his hair and say, *'You can't push everyone away for ever, Nikky. Sooner or later you'll have to let someone in or you'll die alone, like I will.'*

Nikos had always felt a pain in his chest when Alexiou left each time, and had always hoped that he would come back—even though Nikos hadn't seemed to be able to help but do everything in his power to push the man away. But he always had come back. And because Alexiou had never married or had children, Nikos knew that he saw him as a sort of son.

Nikos cursed and turned around, going into his own room. He didn't need this introspection and he certainly didn't welcome it. He needed to take a cold shower and numb the desire and the knot of emotion making his gut tight.

Rome, two days later

Another penthouse apartment at the top of a luxury hotel in one of Rome's most iconic buildings, this time with views of the Colosseum.

Maggie patted Daniel's back where he lay against her shoulder. She shook her head and smiled wryly to herself. If she wasn't careful she would get too used to arriving in a new city with everything she needed laid out for her, a cook to prepare their food and spectacular views. Her walk-in wardrobe was even stocked with clothes again, as it had been in the Athens apartment.

They were here for only one night, before moving on to Madrid tomorrow.

Nikos came into the room behind her. 'I have to go to a meeting now, but I'll be back to take you to the function at six p.m.'

Maggie turned around. She noticed how Nikos's eyes went to Daniel and then away again. He hadn't held him since that first time in Paris. A cold weight settled in her belly. She really didn't want her son growing up with a father who couldn't bond with him…

Nikos frowned. 'Is it too much for you?'

She shook her head and pushed down her concerns. She wanted to make this work. How was Nikos going to bond with his son if he wasn't with him?

'What is the function this evening?' she asked.

'A gala ball to fundraise for a group of charities that help combat homelessness and poverty. The Marchetti Group is its biggest benefactor.'

'Black tie?

He nodded. 'I've arranged for a team from the salon here at the hotel to come up and help get you ready.'

Maggie was simultaneously piqued at his implication that she needed help and relieved. 'Okay, thanks.'

Nikos turned away, and then he turned back. 'What are you going to do today?'

'Marianne and I are going to check out the Colosseum—she's never been, and nor have I.'

'You don't want to go shopping?'

Maggie shook her head. 'Why would I? I have everything I need for me and Daniel here. I'd prefer to see the city.'

* * *

Nikos stood at the vast floor-to-ceiling windows at the Marchetti Group HQ in Rome and took in the view—he could see the Colosseum in the distance. He imagined Maggie walking around the ancient site with Marianne. And the baby most likely in a sling, across her chest.

That feeling of restlessness was back…itching under his skin.

'Nikos?'

The fact that Maggie hadn't wanted to leave Daniel with the nanny and spend the day shopping really shouldn't have surprised him, but it had. It also shouldn't surprise him that she wasn't taking advantage of the fact that she knew he wanted her by using it as a device to manipulate him.

In his world any kind of desire was a weakness to be exploited. And yet she didn't…

'*Nikos?*'

Nikos turned around. The long table was full of board members who were looking at him. He felt exposed. He *never* let a woman compromise his focus—not even his wife.

He sat down at the head of the table and stared down anyone who might doubt his ability to be a member of this group—largely through his own careless actions.

For the first time in his life he regretted the fact that he'd created this persona. His own voice mocked him: *Regrets are for losers.* He could imagine Maggie saying it, teasing him.

Ruthlessly he pushed her image out of his head and said, 'Clearly whatever you were discussing couldn't hold my interest. I suggest you frame it in a more interesting way and start again.'

CHAPTER NINE

'You look...amazing.'

Maggie wanted to blurt out, *Really?* But she forced herself to be gracious and say, 'Thank you—so do you.'

It was true. Nikos was wearing a white tuxedo tonight, with a black bowtie, and he'd never looked more urbane or gorgeous.

'Ready?'

Maggie nodded and walked forward, the long velvet dress moving sinuously around her body. It was high at the front, but completely backless. Which Nikos hadn't noticed yet. Her hair was up in a high ponytail, and she wore clip-on earrings and a sapphire bracelet which matched the blue of the dress.

When she reached Nikos he put a hand on her back to guide her and stopped dead. '*Theos*, Maggie.'

His hand was warm on her back. 'What?'

'Your dress...it's...'

'Backless?'

Nikos gritted his jaw.

Maggie might have felt like giggling if his hand hadn't been having such an effect on her blood. 'The stylist assures me it's perfectly respectable,' she said. She was sure that she'd seen pictures of Nikos escorting women in far less clothing to events.

He said, 'It's fine, We should go.'

In the lift on their way down Maggie could still feel the imprint of his hand against her skin. Awareness of him formed a tight ache in her lower body, which only got worse when he put his hand on her back again to guide her out of the lift and through the hotel lobby.

Resisting him was becoming harder and harder, and right now she wondered how long she could last before she didn't care if he saw her vulnerability or emotion.

A car was waiting outside and they'd soon joined the chaotic Roman traffic to move across the city to the stunning medieval palace where the gala was being held.

Maggie's jaw was almost on the ground as they walked through an open courtyard and into a palatial frescoed room lit by hundreds of candles and chandeliers. Mirrors on the walls reflected the sheer glittering opulence of the room and the people in it.

'This is amazing…' she breathed.

'Is it?' Nikos said, sounding almost bored.

She stopped and looked up at him. 'Are you really so jaded that you can't even appreciate how impressive this is?'

He looked at her. 'More impressive than the Colosseum?'

'Oh, no…well, that was just…mind-boggling. I mean, you'd have to agree that there's nothing quite like it.'

An expression that looked almost wistful crossed his face, and then he plucked two glasses of champagne from a passing waiter's tray, handed her one and said, 'I've never been in it, actually.'

Maggie's jaw dropped again. 'How can you never have visited the Colosseum? What about school trips? There were loads of schoolkids there today.'

Nikos shrugged. 'I had a tutor in Greece and then I was sent to boarding school in England. By the time I got to Rome I was more interested in staking my claim in the business and being a thorn in the side of my father by behaving outrageously than in sightseeing.'

'And after he died?'

Nikos's jaw tightened. 'I had a reputation to live down to and I was working hard.'

Maggie felt an unexpected lump in her throat. She took a quick sip of champagne to push it down.

'Nikos Marchetti! The very man!'

They were interrupted by a tall man who clapped Nikos on the back and looked at Maggie with undisguised interest. Nikos put his hand on her back again and Maggie wanted to groan. How was she going to handle an evening of Nikos touching her bare skin? This dress had been a terrible idea.

'Count Alfredo Pizzoli—please meet my wife, Maggie.'

The man held out his hand. 'A pleasure, my dear. So it wasn't an urban myth, then, your marriage?'

The man guffawed and Nikos said a few more words to him before expertly guiding Maggie deeper into the room, where she was introduced to many more people. This was a very different milieu from Alexiou's friendly and lively Greek birthday party. There was a more cynical edge here.

After a sit-down dinner, and some speeches by various guests about the work that the charities were doing, everyone got up and started milling around.

Nikos stood up and held out a hand for Maggie. He led her towards a room where she could hear soft jazz. It was another ballroom, with a band in the corner on a raised dais. Couples were dancing, bathed in the soft golden light of lots of candles. It was incredibly romantic.

'Like to dance?'

Maggie looked up at Nikos. 'Do I have a choice?'

He led her onto the dance floor even as he said, 'You always have a choice, Maggie.'

Yes, and she'd made a profound one last year, when she'd chosen to succumb to this man's seduction.

Yet even now—finding her way in his world, uncertain about his relationship with Daniel, with *her*—could she regret it? Not for Daniel's sake, obviously. And not even for her own.

Even if he never loves you? asked a voice.

He wants me, she answered herself almost desperately.

He pulled her close against his body, his hand moving over her back, one hand high against his chest. They fitted. Even in high heels her head came to just below his jaw.

And I want him.

Maybe that was enough? She knew she was fighting a losing battle, resisting him. She wanted to sink into him now and let him take her whole weight. So she did—and it was the easiest thing in the world. Too easy...

She looked up at him, admitting wryly, 'I was afraid I was attracted to you because of your charisma and power. My mother always said that was what dazzled her about my father—until she saw what he really was... But after meeting the people here this evening I know it's not that. They have charisma and power, but they're not nice people.'

Nikos's mouth tipped up at one corner. 'Are you saying you like me for *myself*?'

Maggie heard the mocking tone in his voice and ignored it. 'Would that be so bad?'

Tension came into his body. His hand stilled on her back. But his voice was light. 'I keep telling you I'm not that nice.'

'I don't think that's really for you to decide.'

Nikos stopped moving, 'Don't do this, Maggie. Don't think that I'm different from these people. I'm one of them. I come from this world. You're a romantic—you're trying to make me fit into the template you have for a happy future. You *know* I can't promise you that.'

His cynicism rubbed her raw—especially when her whole body ached for fulfilment. 'Don't patronise me, Nikos. Maybe let's just see what kind of future we can have before writing it off, hmm?'

She pushed free of his arms and went to walk away, but her hand was grabbed and she found herself being whirled back into Nikos's arms. It would look as if they were still dancing, but the tension between them was thick.

Before Maggie could do or say anything else Nikos was cupping her jaw and holding her close. And then his mouth was covering hers.

At first Maggie resisted with everything she had. But it was futile. She wanted him too much, and she hated it that knowing he hadn't been with anyone else since here made her desire for him even more potent.

Anger at him for having such a cataclysmic effect on her made her accept his kiss, and she felt a surge of adrenalin rush through them both as she wound her arms around his neck and matched him. Pressing close. Tongues duelling.

They both pulled back at the same moment, breaths coming fast and hard. Hearts pounding.

Nikos just said, 'I want you. *Now*.'

Maggie didn't feel conflicted any more. She felt needy. Aching.

She said the only word she could. 'Yes.'

Nikos took her hand and led her off the dance floor and out through the main ballroom, still thronged with guests. Maggie's cheeks were burning—surely their desire for each other must be glaringly obvious?

They went straight out to where the car was waiting. As soon as Nikos joined her in the back he said something to the driver, who raised the privacy partition before they drove off.

Nikos reached for Maggie, putting his hands around her waist and pulling her towards him so that she was on his lap. Their mouths fused and then Maggie's hands were pushing at his jacket, reaching for his bowtie to undo it but only getting it tangled.

Nikos drew back and huffed out a tortured-sounding laugh. 'Would you believe I'm usually a lot more sophisticated than this?'

Maggie said, 'I don't care.'

Nikos drew her up. 'Pull your dress up and straddle me.'

She did it, knocking her head on the roof of the car. She could feel Nikos's arousal pressing against her and she moved.

He groaned. 'I want to see you…this dress…'

He reached for it at the top and pulled it down from her shoulders, revealing bare breasts that had been supported magically by the boning of the dress. They fell free now…heavy, aching.

Nikos cupped them and licked her nipples, first one and then the other, sending shards of exquisite pleasure down to Maggie's groin. She reached beneath her to Nikos's belt and trousers, fingers clumsy as she tried to release him.

Eventually she rose up and he took her hand away, releasing himself. She could feel his heat and strength and she almost wept with need. The fact that they were in the back of a car, being driven in loops around the city of Rome, was a decadence she couldn't think about now.

Nikos pushed her underwear aside and ran a finger along the seam of her body. She bit her lip— and then she felt the thick head of his erection.

Nikos said something guttural in Greek, but she understood instinctively.

She came down on his length until every hard

inch was embedded in her body. They were both breathing fast. Her hands were on the seat-back behind Nikos as she tried to control her movements, coming slowly up and down again. His hands were on her waist, helping her. It was the most erotic experience of her life and she couldn't last.

Sensing how close she was, Nikos took her, holding her hips as he thrust up. Deeper than before. Harder. And Maggie came, over and over again, barely aware of the warmth of Nikos's explosive release inside her.

She slumped over him, spent. Sated. At peace.

Nikos never wanted to move again.

What the hell was that?

His body was still semi-hard. Still embedded within Maggie's snug embrace. If she moved— *Theos*, he would want her again. Already. The control this woman had over him was not something he wanted to dwell on…

He carefully extricated himself, wincing as the connection between them was broken. Maggie made a little sound that almost had Nikos hauling her back into his arms, but he forced himself to pull her dress up, to hide those magnificent breasts from his gaze.

She moved off his lap and then snuggled into his side like a cat. Nikos had instinctively wrapped his arm around her before he realised that this was the kind of behaviour he'd never indulged in.

Before.

But Maggie was his wife. Things were different now. That was all.

When Maggie woke the next morning she could hear Daniel gurgling in the apartment—presumably with Marianne. She lay on her back for a long moment, reliving the urgency of that coupling in the back of the car.

Nikos had had to carry her in from the car. Her legs had been too weak to hold her up. He'd brought her to her room and she'd been reaching for him again when Daniel had emitted a cry in the room next to hers.

Nikos had been the one to pull back, stand up. 'You should go to him.'

Maggie could only give thanks now that she hadn't exposed herself spectacularly in her ravenous need for *more*.

She turned over and buried her face in the pillow, groaning softly.

A few hours later they were on their way to Madrid—but without Marianne. She'd had to go back to Paris for a minor family emergency and wouldn't be able to join them again until they were in London.

In a way, Maggie was glad of the reprieve. She wouldn't have to attend the event that evening with Nikos. She wouldn't have to try and hide the fact that each outing only seemed to expose her more and more in her growing need for him. Physically and emotionally...

Madrid

Nikos came back to the apartment after midnight. He'd missed Maggie by his side tonight. It unnerved him how quickly he'd become used to her presence. How natural it felt and how unnatural not to have her there.

He opened his tie and the top button of his shirt, shucked off his jacket. He felt restless—a different kind of restlessness from the kind of dissatisfaction that had plagued him for the last few years. He hated to admit it, but it usually dissipated in Maggie's presence.

The way it had dissipated the first time he'd set eyes on her.

He poured himself a shot of whisky and opened the sliding doors that led out to a terrace which looked over the majestic capital city of Spain. He recalled Maggie's awe and wonder at the Roman medieval palace. He could barely remember a time when he'd felt that same kind of awe. He'd been so angry for so long. And since his father had died, he'd focused solely on work and pleasure. Nothing in between.

He heard a sound and tensed. It sounded like a

cry. He went back inside and put his glass down. He heard it again.

Daniel.

Nikos walked down the corridor to the bedrooms and stood outside Maggie's door for a moment. He could hear Daniel gurgling to himself now. Following an instinct he couldn't ignore, he pushed the door open. One low light was on. Maggie was in bed, asleep on her back, hair spread out around her.

Nikos went over and stood by the cot. Daniel was on his back, arms and legs kicking. Eyes wide open. Dark. Nikos put his hand over Daniel's belly and at the same moment the baby smiled up at him. A wide, gummy smile.

Nikos felt as if he was falling. Falling with nothing to cling on to. It was exhilarating and terrifying all at once.

Daniel gurgled again and Nikos looked over at Maggie. She frowned in her sleep. He could see the shadows of tiredness under her eyes even from where he was, and so he did the scariest thing he'd ever done in his life. He put his hands under his son and lifted him up, cradling him against his chest.

He took him out of the bedroom before Maggie could wake, and walked back into the main living area. And then he stood there and looked at his son in his arms. And he felt a kind of awe infuse him, washing aside any hint of restlessness or dissatisfaction.

When Maggie woke she sensed immediately that something was wrong. She looked over and saw that Daniel's cot was empty and jumped out of bed, instantly awake.

Marianne wasn't here and Nikos had gone out. Where could—?

She left the bedroom—and came to a stumbling halt in the doorway leading to the living room.

Nikos was standing on the terrace, just outside the French doors, and she could see Daniel's head in the crook of his arm. Her heart stopped and started again. She was afraid to breathe in case she disturbed the moment.

She could hear Nikos talking to his son in a low voice, in Greek? Italian? Saying…what? She didn't care. The fact that Nikos had actually taken his son in his arms… Her chest felt tight and she put a hand to it. This was huge.

After a moment she walked further into the room and stood in the doorway leading out to the terrace. He must have sensed her presence, as he tensed and turned around.

'He was a awake. I was afraid he'd wake you too.'

Maggie smiled. 'That's okay. Thank you.'

But now, sensing his mother was near, Daniel

let out a cry, and Nikos looked suddenly uncertain. 'What did I do?'

Maggie reached for him. 'Nothing—it's just time for his feed. That's why he was awake. You bought me a few more minutes of sleep.'

Maggie sat down in a nearby chair and undid her nightdress buttons, helping Daniel to latch on without baring too much of her breast. She looked up and saw Nikos had an arrested expression on his face.

She said, 'Would you mind getting me a muslin cloth from the bedroom? There should be some on the nappy changing table near the cot.'

'Of course.'

Nikos left and came back quickly with a couple of cloths. Maggie took them. Nikos sat down on a sofa nearby.

'Do you want me to get you anything else?'

She shook her head. 'No, thanks. How was the event?'

'Not as much fun without you there.'

Maggie's heart hitched. 'I'm sure that's not true.'

They settled into a companionable silence, the sound of Daniel feeding the only thing breaking the silence. It felt intimate in a way that she hadn't felt with Nikos before.

When she'd finished feeding him she put Daniel on her shoulder and stood up. 'I'll put him down again.'

She went back into the bedroom and winded and changed Daniel before putting him down. He was already fast asleep. She felt wide awake now, and couldn't stop thinking about how Nikos had looked at her as she'd fed Daniel.

She'd fully expected that Nikos would have gone to bed, but she found herself going back to the living room. *He was still there.* He was lying on the couch, shoes off. Arm above his head. Was he asleep?

Maggie went over and closed the French doors. Nikos hadn't moved. She couldn't help standing and watching him for a moment, even though she felt like a voyeur. He looked so much younger in sleep…his brow smoothed. She felt an urge to place her fingers against his lips and stepped back before she could do something stupid.

But as she was turning away her hand was caught.

'Where do you think you're going?' His voice was a rough growl.

'I thought you were asleep.'

Nikos tugged her down onto the couch beside him. He came up on one elbow. She could feel his gaze on her as he brought his hand up and flicked open the couple of buttons on her nightdress that she'd just closed.

It had to be the most un-erotic piece of clothing—a white cotton nightdress with buttons strategically placed to make it easy to breast-feed—but suddenly it felt like the most provocative thing in the world.

Nikos looked at her as he put his hand underneath the cotton to cup her breast. She sucked in a breath. It was still sensitive after feeding. But deliciously so.

He brought his hand up then, catching her hair and looping it around his fingers, tugging her down towards him until she was flat against his chest and her mouth hovered above his. Their breaths intermingled. He was like steel underneath her.

'Do you want this, Maggie?'

It freaked her out how much she wanted him. All the time.

She nodded.

He reached up and their mouths touched. She groaned. He speared her hair with his hands, angling her to make the kiss deeper, more explicit. Maggie wanted to rub herself against him like a needy cat.

Urgency gripped them both. Nikos pulled back for a second, grabbed her hips and pulled her on top of him so that her thighs fell either side of his hips. She wasn't wearing any underwear. He reached down and found this out for himself. They both gasped.

Maggie unbuttoned his shirt, needing to feel his chest. Nikos undid his trousers, lifting himself up to pull them down. And then she felt him there, released and hot and hard against her hungry flesh.

He opened the rest of the buttons on her nightdress, releasing her breasts into his hands, and she rose over him and took him in her hand as she guided herself onto his rigid length.

Her hands were spread on his chest as she rode him, tentatively at first and then with more confidence, biting her lip against the spasm of pleasure as he touched a point deep inside her.

He massaged her breasts, coming up to take one nipple and then the other into his mouth. That sent her into a frenzy, and her movements became less slick, more frantic, as she chased the peak that teased her...

She must have sobbed, or pleaded or something, because Nikos clamped his hands on her hips and took control, holding her still while he thrust into her over and over again until she collapsed against him and pressed her mouth to his in a desperate kiss, pleading silently for him to stop and yet never to stop.

And then it came—the moment when everything went still and taut before a quickening rush of pleasure so intense that she could only submit to its power and wait for the storm to pass.

When Maggie woke the next morning she was back in her bed, with only the vaguest memory of Nikos carrying her there. Daniel was awake and kicking his legs happily in his cot. She lay there for a moment, wondering if actually that had been a particularly intense dream last night.

But, no. Her body was tender in secret places.

She turned on her side and looked at Daniel, recalled seeing him in Nikos's arms. Emotion gripped her again. And something almost fearful.

The force of need she felt around Nikos and the fact that it wasn't diminishing was overwhelming. She'd heard that desire burnt itself out eventually, but this didn't feel as if it would *ever* burn out. For her. But would it for Nikos?

Of course it would. It had to be a fluke that he still wanted her. Some weird aberration.

He hasn't slept with anyone else since you.

She hated that voice in her head, making her think of things like that. Things that gave her hope. That made her wish for other things, like a proper relationship with Nikos—not separate bedrooms and moments snatched while they were on this whistlestop tour around Europe.

Once the tour was over...when things calmed down...surely then things would settle into a routine? Although *Nikos* and *routine* didn't really go together. He seemed very much at home with this peripatetic existence, but Maggie knew she couldn't live like this on a regular basis.

But maybe now...maybe now that he seemed to want to bond with Daniel...things could change?

* * *

Maggie laughed and Daniel gurgled. 'Honestly—he won't break. Just take his legs together in your hand and lift him up…good…then wipe his bottom with the baby wipe. That's it. Make sure it's dry and clean. Put the nappy here…'

The concentration on Nikos's face as he mastered the art of changing a nappy was nothing short of comical. It told Maggie a lot more about him than she'd bet he would ever want anyone to know.

He placed Daniel down on the clean nappy and pulled it up between his legs, then secured it over his belly with the sticky tapes on the sides.

'I did it!'

After about ten attempts.

Maggie didn't say it out loud. Daniel had been amazingly patient. As if he'd sensed his father was trying to make an effort.

'You did.'

Nikos pulled on Daniel's Babygro and secured the buttons, then scooped up his son, carefully supporting his head, and walked out into the apartment with him.

Marianne was standing in the doorway and she sent Maggie an expressive look. Maggie returned it, with a smile and a small shrug, and followed Nikos out. The other woman had just arrived back from Paris, so hadn't yet witnessed Nikos's new interest in his son.

Maggie knew she shouldn't really be surprised that someone as focused as Nikos was taking to his role as a father with an expert zeal and a speed that left her breathless. They'd arrived in London earlier that day, and on the plane over from Madrid he'd fed Daniel from a bottle. And winded him. And when Daniel had vomited down Nikos's back he hadn't even cared. He'd just changed his shirt.

And then, on their drive to the hotel from the airport, she'd overheard him rescheduling a meeting for later in the day so he could come with them to the apartment and spend some time with Daniel.

Nikos turned around with his big hand across Daniel's back. 'Hyde Park is nearby—we could go for a walk and get a coffee?'

Maggie tried to tamp down the surge of happiness. 'Sure... If you have time?'

'Of course I have time.'

They went out with Daniel in his compact pram. The temperatures were starting to turn cooler after the summer and there was a freshness in the air. There was also, although Maggie hated even to think it, a sense of hope.

When they'd walked through the park for a while, and found a place to sit down and have coffee—decaf for her—she said, 'So what's on the agenda this evening?'

He took a sip of espresso. 'It's the opening of

a new designer store on Bond Street—one of our labels.'

He mentioned the iconic name and Maggie's eyes widened. It was a byword in extreme luxe fashion—one of the most timeless brands in the world.

'That's one of yours?'

Nikos nodded. 'It won't be that formal an event, though. It's just a party to welcome the new head designer.'

Immediately Maggie felt anxious. 'What does that mean? What should I wear?'

Nikos looked wicked. 'Something very short and very sparkly.'

CHAPTER TEN

THANKS TO THE stylist at the boutique in the London M Group hotel Maggie had been able to fulfil Nikos's brief, and when they arrived at the event on Bond Street she was wearing a very short and sparkly green dress paired with vertiginous heels. He'd instructed her to leave her hair down.

Maggie clung to Nikos's hand as they ran the gauntlet of photographers lining each side of the short red carpet. They were calling her name as well as Nikos's now.

'Maggie, love, over here!'

'Maggie! Pose for us!'

'Who are you wearing?'

Thankfully an award-winning actress appeared behind her and their focus shifted to her.

When they got inside the noise faded and was replaced by chatter and pulsing music. The store was cavernous—more like a gallery space than a shop.

Maggie was still clinging to Nikos's hand. She let go, embarrassed. 'I wasn't expecting them to call out my name. It feels weird that they know who I am.'

He looked at her. He was darkly sophisticated tonight, in a dark blue suit and white shirt, no tie. Shirt open at the neck. 'They just call out your name to get a reaction. You'll get used to it.'

She didn't really relish the thought of this kind of experience becoming a regular feature in her life. But she shelved her concerns. More than any other event they'd been to, this one was seriously star-studded. Actresses, supermodels, politicians... She'd even spotted a very popular ex-American President and his wife.

She sensed Nikos tense beside her, and then a familiar face appeared. 'Maks!' she said.

He bent towards her to give her a kiss on the cheek. 'Maggie, how are you? Still putting up with my brother?'

Maggie heard the mocking tone in his voice— not unlike his brother's. 'Well, it *has* only been a couple of weeks...'

He looked from her to his brother. 'Nikos.'

'Maks.'

Maggie lamented the tension between the brothers. It made her heart ache to see how similar they were, to know how much they'd missed out on not growing up together.

Maks said, 'You didn't show for the board meeting today.'

'I was busy.'

'Luckily for you the wholesome pictures circulating of you and your new family seem to have done wonders for our stock prices.'

Maggie was confused. 'Pictures?'

Maks took out his phone and showed her a tabloid news site. There were pictures of them in Hyde Park from only a few hours ago, underneath a headline: *Reformed playboy spends afternoon with new family. How long before he gets bored?*

Maggie felt sick.

Nikos said something to Maks that sounded like a snarl and took her hand, pulling her away. They moved into the crowd and Maggie desperately tried to push out of her mind the insidious suspicion that Nikos had engineered that trip to the park specifically for a photo opportunity.

She'd seen the way he looked at Daniel. The way he was bonding with him when no one was watching. She had to give him the benefit of the doubt and trust him. Give them a chance.

He stopped a waiter and asked her what she wanted to drink. She pasted a bright smile on her face. 'Just sparkling water, please. I have to feed Daniel later.'

Nikos took champagne. 'Okay?' he asked.

She looked up. She longed to ask him if he'd gone out with her today knowing they'd be photographed, but at the last second she said, 'Fine.'

After that they were sucked into a round of introductions and conversations that Maggie did her best to keep up with. But she couldn't deny she was tired. Travelling with a small breastfeeding baby was catching up on her, and at one stage, when Nikos had been spirited away by an assistant to meet someone, she couldn't hide a huge yawn.

'I don't blame you—these events bore me to tears too.'

She turned to find Maks beside her. He looked at her assessingly.

'Nikos seems different...less distracted. Maybe you and the baby will be good for him and the business. I'm sorry I showed you those pictures, it was unecessary.'

Maggie made a face. 'That's ok, I probably would have seen them anyway. What about you? Do *you* want a family?'

Maks's expression turned grim, the bones in his face standing out starkly. 'No intention of it. In fact I'm glad Nikos has done us all a favour in that regard.'

Maggie said, as lightly as she could, 'You never know. I don't think it was Nikos's intention either, but...' She blushed. 'Things happen.' She coughed, mortified that the conversation had taken this turn.

The grim expression faded from Maks's face and he looked at her again. 'Did you know it's Nikos's birthday tomorrow?'

She shook her head, realising there was still so much she didn't know. 'No.'

Maks said, 'In a funny twist of fate—or not so funny—all of us three half-brothers have birthdays in the same month. Nikos is first, then Sharif, and me at the end.'

'And your sister Sasha? Is she here tonight?'

'God, no—you couldn't pay Sasha to come to an event like this. No, her birthday is in spring.'

Then Maks's expression changed again, his eyes narrowing on someone across the room. He muttered almost to himself, 'What the hell is *she* doing here?'

Then he was gone, cutting a swathe through the crowd before Maggie could see who he was talking about.

Nikos reappeared. 'I saw you talking to Maks again—he didn't upset you?'

'No, actually, he was sweet.'

Nikos made a rude sound. 'I wouldn't have ever described Maks as *sweet*.'

'He apologised for showing me the pictures.' Maggie looked at Nikos carefully, but he showed no sign of discomfort or guilt.

'Did you know there would be photographers in the park?'

Nikos shrugged. 'I guess I took it for granted that they might be. Does it bother you?'

'Of course it bothers me that we can't go for

a walk without being photographed. That's not normal.'

He shook his head. 'It's normal for us now.'

Maggie felt angry at his laissez-faire attitude. She stood directly in front of him.

'Does it have to be, though? Just because you all grew up under the glare of the media, it doesn't mean your own child has to. I don't want Daniel living his life in a fishbowl. He deserves as normal an existence as we can give him. Plenty of rich and famous people have families and manage to keep them out of the public eye.'

Nikos was taken aback by Maggie's passion. She looked like a warrior mother, protecting her young. The kind of champion he'd never had.

An unexpected and unwelcome surge of emotion made him suddenly reject the thought of Daniel being subjected to what he'd experienced. 'You're right. There's no reason why we can't live differently—or at least do our best to.'

She arched a brow. 'Even if pictures of a happy family outing are good for your stock prices?'

Nikos's conscience pricked. He'd taken more than Maggie's innocence.

But he forced himself to say lightly, 'Now who's being cynical?'

The following evening Maggie was nervous. The next day they were due to travel to the South of

France and nothing had been scheduled for tonight. Except *this*. The thing that was making
her nervous.

When Maggie heard the sound of the door she
and Marianne quickly lit the candles on the cake
and waited for Nikos to appear. As soon as he did
they both started singing *Happy Birthday*—but
they trailed to a halt at the look of utter horror
on his face.

He looked at Maggie and she'd never seen him
so haunted. 'What the hell is *this*? How did you
know it was my birthday?'

'Maks told me last night,' Maggie replied. 'I
baked you a cake.'

'He shouldn't have told you.'

Nikos turned and left the room and Maggie
looked at Marianne, beyond bewildered.

Nikos couldn't breathe. He pulled at his tie,
opened a couple of buttons. But that tight fist was
around his chest, squeezing tighter and tighter.

He rested his hands heavily on the desk,
breathed as deeply as he could, exactly as his
friend had told him—an ex-French Foreign Le-
gionnaire who had looked at him one day and
said, 'How long have you been having panic attacks?'

That friend had known because he'd recognised the signs.

To Nikos's surprise, the symptoms started to

fade—far more quickly than they usually did. He straightened up and went over to the window that looked out over London.

The shock and horror of seeing that cake, lit with candles, and then Maggie and Marianne singing… It was quite literally his worst nightmare. But for a tiny, treacherous moment he'd been transported back in time to *before* the day had become tainted for ever.

He never mentioned his birthday. He never acknowledged it. Why the hell had Maks told her?

Because his brother didn't know.

There was a soft knock on his study door. He tensed.

The door opened. 'Nikos? Are you okay?'

Nikos felt conflicting things. He wanted to snarl at Maggie to leave him alone and yet he wanted her to come in, so that he could pull her close and lose himself in her scent and silky body.

He bit out, 'I'm fine,' and went over to his drinks cabinet to pour himself a measure of whisky.

He was aware of her coming in. Wearing jeans and a T-shirt. Hair down. She could wear a sack and he'd want her. The desire wasn't burning out. It was burning up.

'Nikos…?'

Even her voice was enough to distract him, make him clench down low to try and control his body's response.

He said curtly, 'I'm sorry. You weren't to know.'

'Know what?'

He turned around. 'That I despise my birthday and any mention of it.'

She sat back against his desk as if winded. 'Why?'

Why, indeed?

Nikos walked over to the window, his back towards Maggie. His own face was reflected to him. Distorted.

He said, 'I never even knew it was my birthday until I was about five and my father turned up in Athens to take me out to a restaurant. There was more cake and sweets than I'd ever seen in my life—my grandparents didn't allow sweet things. My father encouraged me to eat my fill. I thought he had come to take me home with him. I was so happy.

'But I'd eaten too much cake, and I started to be sick. My father was naturally disgusted and sent me home with my nanny. I was sick for a week and I thought that was why he hadn't taken me home with him… Then, every year on my birthday he would show up and take me to a restaurant and order cake—even though I'd developed an aversion to it after my first experience.

'I came to dread the annual event, even as I lived in hope that he would take me away with him. But he never did. He would just put me back in the car and send me back to my grandparents' villa, to be sick for a week. That cake came to symbolise his disregard…the perpetual disappointment.

'And then one year he took me out and told me that he was taking me away. I thought he was finally taking me home with him. I knew he had a new wife and a son and a daughter—Maks and Sasha—and I was ecstatic at the thought of siblings. I was so lonely at my grandparents' house… But he didn't take me to tmeet hem. He took me to boarding school. One of the most remote schools in England.

'I never saw my grandparents again. They couldn't have cared less. And my father didn't visit me on my birthday any more. I discovered that my birthday is also the date of my mother's death. She killed herself on my second birthday.'

He turned around then, to face Maggie. Her face was pale, blue eyes huge.

'So that's why I have an aversion to birthdays, and anything sweet.'

Maggie stood up. 'Nikos, your father was some kind of sadist—and as for your grandparents… they didn't deserve the title. They rejected their own daughter and then you.' She came closer. 'I'm sorry. If I'd known—'

'How could you?' His voice was harsh. He modulated it. 'You couldn't have known. No one knows. Not even my brothers.'

She bit her lip and pulled something out of her back pocket. An envelope.

Nikos looked at it suspiciously. 'What is it?'

She pushed it towards him. 'A present.'

Nikos shook his head. He wanted to push it back. 'You don't have to give me anything.'

No one had ever given him anything.

'Please.'

Nikos took it reluctantly and opened it. It was a card with a nice bucolic scene.

Maggie said, 'It reminded me of the garden at Kildare House.'

Nikos opened it. Inside there was some kind of a printout. He picked it out and read it and his chest felt tight again. It was a voucher for a personal tour of the Colosseum.

Maggie said quickly, 'We can do it the next time we're in Rome—or, you know, whenever…'

Nikos saw a message on the card.

Happy Birthday, Nikos
Maggie and Daniel
XX

He put the card and the voucher down. He felt light-headed after revealing more than he'd ever revealed to anyone.

'You're sweet, Maggie. Too sweet for me.'

I can't have sweet things.

She shook her head. 'I'm not too sweet—I'm

just not as hardened and cynical as everyone else you know. I'm normal, Nikos. Most people out there are like me.'

No, she was more than that. Most people weren't as sweet as her. She was unique, and Nikos knew that he had no right to any of Maggie's sweetness. And yet he'd gorged himself on her.

He felt toxic.

'Go back and enjoy the cake with Marianne. Thank you, but it's not for me.'

Maggie felt a chill go down her back. Nikos was more remote than she'd ever seen him. He'd retreated to some place she knew she couldn't reach.

She moved towards him and he stepped back. A sharp pain lanced her gut.

'We'll be having dinner soon, if you want to join us.'

Your family.

Nikos shook his head abruptly. 'I don't need dinner. I have calls to make before our trip to France.'

The villa that Nikos had hired in the south of France was jaw-droppingly impressive, hugging the edge of a steep hill with views over the Mediterranean. A thoroughly modern structure, it was white and steel and sleek and impossibly sexy.

Maggie hated it.

And she was tired after a sleepless night with Daniel.

She and Marianne had decided that at almost four months he was starting to teethe—which had to be the reason for his tetchy humour and the fact that he would only take milk from her breast. He wasn't interested in a bottle.

Marianne was looking after Daniel now, in between feeds.

Nikos appeared on the terrace and Maggie had to steel herself not to react. But it was even harder today, when he was in faded worn jeans and a white polo shirt which showed off the olive tones of his skin and his musculature.

He barely looked at her, though, and glanced at his watch. 'Staff are coming to set up soon and the guests will be arriving from five p.m. I've arranged for a team to come up from a salon in Cannes. Clothes have been ordered—they should be in your wardrobe.'

'Yes, they're there.'

She'd seen the glittering array of dresses. Each one as beautiful and intimidating as the next. Even though she was getting used to the process she still felt like a fish out of water—and even more so now, when she was feeling fatigued and concerned about Daniel.

'Are you okay?' Nikos asked.

Maggie looked at him. She felt like asking if

he really cared. He'd barely said two words to her since that conversation in his study in London. But now probably wasn't the time to get into anything.

'I'm fine, just a bit tired. And Daniel—'

Nikos frowned. 'Is he okay?'

'He's fine—we think he's starting to teethe.'

'Is that serious? Does he need a doctor?'

Maggie smiled. 'No, it's not serious—it's perfectly normal. All babies teethe. It just makes them cranky.'

'Let me know if it's anything more. Maybe you shouldn't come this evening—maybe you should stay with Daniel?'

Maggie smarted at the suggestion that she should absent herself. Which was crazy. Obviously Daniel was more important, but—ridiculously—she felt jealous of her own baby, who seemed to be commanding Nikos's attention with more skill than she did.

Earlier, on the plane, she hadn't been able to soothe a fractious Daniel. Nikos had put down his papers and held out his arms. 'Here, let me try.'

Almost immediately the little traitor had stopped crying and promptly fallen asleep in his father's arms.

It was something that should have sparked joy within Maggie. Alleviating her worst fears. But instead it had made her feel redundant. If Daniel and Nikos bonded, where did that leave *her*? She hadn't ever anticipated that scenario.

The suspicion that he was punishing her for intruding—going too far with the birthday celebration—was like acid in her stomach. A man as proud as Nikos wouldn't thank her after telling her the sorry facts of his lonely childhood.

She forced those thoughts out of her mind. 'Daniel will be fine. Marianne is with him and I can feed him when I need to.'

'I'll leave it up to you—just don't feel obliged.'

Maggie watched as he walked off. So now it didn't even matter if his wife was by his side? When it was supposed to be part of the reason for this marriage…? She couldn't escape the feeling that the ground was shifting underneath her and she had nothing to cling on to.

A few hours later Maggie looked at herself critically in the mirror. Make-up had covered the circles under her eyes, but she knew she still looked a bit washed out.

Her hair was caught back in a low bun and she wore a strapless light blue sheath dress, down to the knee, with matching sandals with kitten heels that were mercifully easy to walk in.

She left a sleeping Daniel with Marianne and went downstairs, nervous of Nikos's reaction now that he was in this strange aloof mood. He turned as she came down and she saw the flare of something in his eyes before his face became impassive again. She felt a treacherous little flicker of hope.

He hadn't appreciated having to open up. That was all it was.

'Is this okay?'

'It's fine.' His voice was gruff.

He wore a steel-grey suit and no tie. Casual, but elegant. And unashamedly masculine.

Staff had been busy in the interim. They'd decorated the space with flowers and she could see a long table outside in the shade, set for dinner.

A new scent infused the air. She wrinkled her nose, 'Is that—?'

Nikos grimaced. 'Yes, that's the new perfume—a little overpowering, but it's one of our biggest sellers already.'

Maggie saw cars starting to appear in the driveway, and as everyone arrived she got split up from Nikos. She did her best to mingle and make small talk with people, but found that this crowd looked at her as if she were a curiosity, and seemed more interested in speaking behind her back when she walked away.

She caught more than a few snide glances from other women. And one woman looked at her and openly laughed. To Maggie's intense shame, she was transported back in time to when the girls and boys at her school would laugh at her and call her *Beanpole*. And even though she wasn't the tallest woman here, in this place, that old feeling of exposure was hot and crippling and immediate.

She had a sense of having been found out. She was a fraud. She wasn't from this world and they knew it. She didn't belong here—she would never belong here. And that was the realisation Nikos had come to too. The only thing keeping them together now was—

Suddenly Nikos was there, looking at her. Specifically at her breasts. He came forward and took her arm, leading her to one side.

'What is that? Did you spill something?'

'What's what?'

Maggie looked down and groaned. There were two wet patches over her breasts. She was leaking milk. She'd ignored the signs of her breasts growing tingly and heavy, too intent on making a good impression at the party. Now she'd made an impression, all right.

Mortified, she said, 'I need to feed Daniel.'

She pulled away from Nikos and hurried upstairs, conscious of whispers and muffled laughter. Face burning, she went into the bedroom.

Marianne took one look and handed her Daniel, saying, 'I'll find you another dress.'

Maggie undid her dress and settled Daniel on her breast, taking a look down at the terrace, where all those honeyed people were milling about.

She shook her head when Marianne came back

in with an armful of clothes. 'No way. I'm not going back down there—they're piranhas.'

Marianne made a huffing sound. 'He needs you.'

Maggie could see Nikos, head and shoulders above everyone else. Surrounded by sycophants.

'Does he? I don't think he does, Marianne. And clearly I'm not really suited to this milieu.'

Marianne said enigmatically, 'All the more reason for you to go back down and remind him of that.'

The last thing Maggie wanted to do was expose herself to that snooty crowd's ridicule again, but she wasn't that shy, over-tall girl any more. She was a woman. A wife and a mother. And she'd made a pledge to honour her husband even if theirs wasn't a love match. *And never would be.*

So when Maggie had fed and changed Daniel and put him down, she changed into a black silk maxi-dress and flat sandals. She shook her hair loose, put on some red lipstick and went back to the party.

All the guests were sitting at the long dining table. Waiters were serving. Nikos was at the head. As one, everyone seemed to stop and look at her when she appeared on the terrace. For an awful moment Maggie thought she couldn't do it—and then Nikos stood up and held out a hand.

'Everyone, if you haven't yet met her, this is my wife, Maggie.'

She walked towards him, his gold and green eyes holding her. Whatever was going on with him, and this new distance he was putting between them, she would be grateful for ever for this show of solidarity.

She sat down at his right-hand side and the woman on her right put a hand on her arm. Maggie looked around warily, to see the friendly face of a woman a bit older than her.

She said, 'Oh, my God—I felt so sorry for you. The exact same thing happened to me at a function after I had my first baby—in front of hundreds of people.' She stuck out her hand. 'I'm Melissa, and this is my husband Klaus—he's one of the chief parfumiers in the company.'

Maggie smiled with relief and shook her hand, confiding, 'I almost didn't come back down.'

Melissa said, *sotto voce*, 'I'm glad you did. Those women don't deserve a second thought— they're just insanely jealous that you've managed to tame one of the world's most notorious playboys.'

Maggie smiled weakly. *Had* she tamed Nikos? No… But maybe Daniel had. The problem was, she suspected Nikos was already chafing at the reality of being tamed.

Later that night, Maggie woke up with a start. She'd fallen asleep in the chair where she'd fed Daniel, who was now back in his cot, fast asleep. She'd come up to feed him after dinner.

She stood up and went to the window which overlooked the terrace. All was quiet now, the guests all departed. Her insides clenched when she saw the lone figure of Nikos, looking out over the view. It made her heart ache—especially now that she knew just how bleak his childhood had been.

She wanted to go down to him and slide her arms around his waist, offer him comfort. But she knew he wouldn't welcome it. That image belonged to a different scenario. One in which Nikos actually cared for her. Like she cared for him.

Loved him.

Her breath stopped as that cataclysmic realisation sank in. She loved him. Desperately. Futilely. And he couldn't have made it clearer that her affection wasn't welcome.

Monte Carlo was as tiny and picturesque as Maggie had always imagined. In her teens she'd been fascinated with Grace Kelly, and had read everything about her, so to be here now was overwhelming.

They'd taken a helicopter from Cannes, landing on a helipad near the Marchetti Group hotel where they had an exclusive suite. The hotel was part of the opulent casino where they were due to attend an event that night.

This last event of the tour was a charity auction in aid of all the charities that the Marchetti Group supported. Afterwards there was to be a high-stakes poker game with all the proceeds going to charity.

Once again a team had come up from the hotel salon and they'd transformed Maggie into a far sleeker version of herself. Her hair lay in waves over one bare shoulder. Her cocktail dress was black and asymmetrical, one-shouldered, down to the knee with a slit up one side.

Nikos walked into the living area of the suite, doing up his cufflinks. He looked up and that dark gaze swept her up and down. If there was a flare of interest in his eyes she didn't see it. She felt cold.

'How's Daniel?' he asked.

'Fine—fed and changed. Marianne has taken him out for a stroll around the gardens. I've expressed some milk, so we shouldn't have a recurrence of—'

Nikos shook his head. 'Don't worry about that.'

She took a step towards him. 'Look, Nikos, is everything…okay between us?'

He put his hands in his pockets. 'Why wouldn't it be?'

Maggie bit her lip. 'It just feels like since London… Maybe you didn't want to tell me…' She trailed off.

'Everything is fine.'

Except it wasn't. There was a cold chasm between them. Even as her blood still hummed just at being near him. She hated the insidious feeling that he didn't want her any more.

He said, 'Ready?'

She nodded and walked towards him. As they left the suite she said, 'I presume once we're back in Paris things will calm down?'

The lift attendant greeted them and pressed the button for the ground floor.

Nikos looked at her. 'What do you mean?'

'Well, there won't be so much travelling…we can get settled.'

The lift doors opened and they got out.

Nikos said warningly. 'I do travel a lot. I can't say I don't. You won't always have to come with me, but your presence will be required.'

Maggie envisaged all those events with a stony Nikos by her side. 'I know that. But as Daniel grows into a toddler, and then older, he'll need a more regular routine.'

'That's what nannies are for.'

His easy response sent a spurt of anger up her spine. She faced him. 'After everything you told me the other day, you'd entrust our son's care to a *nanny*? Do you envisage sending him to boarding school too?'

Now his eyes flashed—but it gave Maggie no satisfaction.

Nikos took her hand. She tried to pull away

but he wouldn't let her. 'We will not have this conversation here.'

Maggie dug her heels in. 'When, then?'

Nikos gritted his jaw. 'Later. After the event.'

Maggie noticed that people were waiting for them, so she let Nikos lead her towards them. They were swept into the ballroom—a magnificent baroque space, with open French doors and a terrace leading down to stunning gardens. A small orchestra played classical music on the terrace and Maggie accepted a small glass of champagne, feeling a little reckless from that rush of adrenalin just now.

But as she stood by Nikos's side and the auction got underway, the adrenalin faded and she'd never felt more alone. In the space of only two weeks, it was scary how used she'd got to him touching her, checking to see if she was okay.

But now it was as if he couldn't bring himself to look at her, never mind touch her. As if he wouldn't even notice if she left.

So she did.

CHAPTER ELEVEN

NIKOS KNEW THE moment Maggie walked away. He knew he was behaving like a boor. But he couldn't stop. When she'd asked him earlier if things were okay—when she'd mentioned London—he'd felt that awful sense again that he was toxic, and that with every moment spent in his company she was being tainted by him.

In truth, he was finding it hard even to look at Maggie, even though he burned for her more than ever. Looking at her...at those blue eyes... made him feel exposed down to his core.

Daniel was the only one who seemed to look at him and not expect anything.

That's because he's a baby.

Nikos scowled at himself. But the utter trust which with Daniel looked at him soothed something inside him. Something that Maggie rubbed up against. Making him remember...too much. Making him want things he couldn't have. Sweetness. Light.

Maggie hadn't returned by the time the auction was over. He sensed instinctively that she wouldn't. He'd pushed her away.

He told himself he was glad. She needed to know what he was like.

The ghost of his past whispered around him, beckoning to him. Reminding him of his worth. His true worth. Maggie had made him feel as if he might be worth something—something more—but it had been an illusion.

She saw too much. She wanted too much. He could feel it from her. A silent plea. One that he couldn't possibly fulfil.

It was far better that she remembered who he was and who he could never be. Before she got hurt.

When Maggie woke she had a crick in her neck. She realised that she'd fallen asleep in an awkward position on the bed after feeding Daniel— again. She padded out of the bedroom to find Marianne still awake, reading in the living area.

'Has Nikos come back?'

Marianne shook her head. 'Not yet.' Then she frowned. 'Are you okay?'

'Sure… Why?'

'I heard you…being sick.'

Maggie flushed with guilt. She'd been feeling nauseous all day. 'It was nothing.'

Marianne looked at her. 'Have you started your periods again?'

Maggie shook her head. 'No, so it can't possibly be—' She stopped talking, a clammy, panicky feeling washing through her. She looked at Marianne. 'It couldn't be…could it?'

Marianne stood up, her expression serious. 'I'm not sure, but I don't think a lack of periods or breastfeeding is foolproof protection.'

Maggie wanted to sit down. Was it possible? Could she be pregnant again? Already?

She remembered with Daniel that her morning sickness had been worst in the evenings. She felt sick again.

She forced a smile. 'I'm sure it's not… Would you watch Daniel if I go out for a minute?'

'Of course.'

It was only when the lift reached the ground floor that Maggie realised she'd forgotten to put on her shoes. But it was quiet down here. The ballroom was empty now, bathed in moonlight, staff were packing up chairs.

She spotted a person she recognised as being one of Nikos's assistants and asked him where Nikos was. He led her to another room, where a scary-looking bouncer opened the door.

Maggie gasped. It was a whole other world. It was like a scene from a James Bond movie. There was a bar and a raised dais, where men and women sat around an oval table. This must be the high-stakes poker game.

Nikos was there. Bowtie undone. Sleeves rolled up. There was something incredibly weary about him that caught at her before she could chase it away. Nikos didn't need her concern and he wouldn't welcome it.

He wasn't smoking, but a cloud of cigar smoke hung in the air. Maggie waved a hand in front of her face to clear it. Nikos looked up and saw her—and there it was. The flare. Before he blanked his expression again.

But it must have been her imagination. She knew something had been irrevocably broken between them.

He sat back in his chair. 'Ladies and gentlemen—my wife, Maggie.'

Everyone turned and looked at her. She blushed and glared at Nikos.

He stood up. 'Come join me. I need good luck.'

Against her better instincts Maggie went over and climbed the steps. Nikos reached for her and sat down again, pulling her into his lap. Her bones liquefied. His thighs were like steel. He hadn't touched her since Madrid and she could feel the ever-present need. Embarrassing.

She held herself rigid.

He wrapped his arms around her and said, 'Ladies and gentlemen, I can highly recommend getting married—I'm a transformed man.'

His mocking tone was too much. Maggie didn't like it—and she didn't like Nikos's volatile energy.

She stood up, but he pulled her down again. 'Don't go… I need you.'

She looked at him and said, for his ears only, 'You don't need me—that's the problem.'

She stood up again.

'I just wanted to make sure you were all right.'

She went back down the steps and he said from behind her, 'Don't wait up.'

She turned and looked at him. It was as if he'd morphed back into that louche playboy she'd first met.

'I won't,' she said. And left.

Dawn was rising outside when Nikos returned to the suite. It was quiet. He felt hollowed out. Like a husk. He threw down his coat and heard a sound. He looked up. Maggie was standing by the window.

She was wearing jeans and a long-sleeved top. Her hair was up in a messy knot. She looked tired. Pale. There was a jacket on the chair beside her. Daniel was in his baby seat, asleep.

'What's going on? Why are you up?'

Maggie lifted her chin and something about that tiny movement threatened to break something apart inside Nikos. But he clamped down on it. Hard.

'We're getting an early flight back to Ireland, via London. I'm just waiting for a taxi. Marianne is in bed asleep. She's going to go back to Paris later—she's taking a holiday until we figure out what we're doing.'

Nikos shook his head, a cold feeling spreading through him. 'What are you talking about?'

She said, 'You told me we'd talk about things after the event, but you stayed out all night.'

Even though Nikos knew he'd precipitated this very scenario, something that felt like desperation and panic curdled in his gut. 'So let's talk now.'

She shook her head. 'It's too late. This isn't working, Nikos. Daniel is my priority and he's starting to teethe. He needs to be in one place—not moving around. The apartment in Paris isn't suitable. We need a home, and clearly you're not ready to change your life to accommodate that if last night is anything to go by.'

Nikos felt a sense of futility wash over him. This was what he wanted. Maggie was too close. She saw too much. She needed to get away from him.

'What will you do?' Nikos asked.

Maggie fought to hold on to her composure even as she broke apart inside. He wasn't even putting up a fight.

'We'll go back to Kildare House, if that's okay?'

'That house is yours, Maggie. I gave it to you in the pre-nuptial agreement. It's yours no matter what happens.'

'You did?' She'd barely read the agreement. She was momentarily speechless but then it hit her—he cared so little about the house he was prepared to give it to her.

Stiffly, she said, 'I'll accept it on Daniel's behalf.'

'It's *yours*.'

Nikos sounded almost angry.

Maggie knew she should walk away now, but a rebellious part of her needed to push Nikos… push him all the way to articulating just how little hope there was. Because she knew if there was any doubt she would never rest easy.

She forced herself to ask. 'What else is mine, Nikos?'

His eyes narrowed on her. 'What do you want?'

This was it. A terrifying leap of faith. But she had no choice.

'It's not *what* I want—it's *who*. You, Nikos. I want *you*. All of you. I've fallen in love with you, in spite of all your warnings. Because you let me in to see someone that no one else knows. And I think you're pushing me away because of that… aren't you?'

She held her breath.

Nikos's face was pale. 'Don't be ridiculous.'

She walked over to him. There was stubble on his jaw. His weariness was palpable. She knew she was risking everything by doing this, but perhaps it was the only way to kill the flicker of hope that might destroy her.

'I know you want me, Nikos, and I think you

feel something for me—maybe not love, but more than like.'

A harsh expression came over his face. '*Not* more than like! I told you I couldn't offer more than that. And as for wanting you? Desire always fades in the end.'

Maggie absorbed the cruel blow of his words and stepped closer. She put a hand to the back of his head, urging his head down.

Nikos was stiff. 'What are you doing?'

She pressed her mouth to his before she could lose her nerve, almost forgetting why she was doing it as his scent filled her nostrils and she felt those firm contours. She flicked out her tongue, tasting the seam of his lips. She could feel his tension.

Nikos jerked back and put his hands on her arms, pushed her back. 'Don't embarrass yourself, Maggie.'

He really didn't want her any more.

She faltered. Lost her nerve.

She'd just exposed herself spectacularly and Nikos hadn't crumbled.

She went on wooden legs to put on her jacket, picked up Daniel's baby seat.

She walked back to Nikos and forced herself to look into his impassive face. 'You know where we'll be. I need to do what's best for my son now.'

All the way to the door her treacherous heart

hoped that he would try and stop her...tell her it had all been a huge mistake. But he didn't.

Nikos walked over to the window and looked down into the main courtyard. After a few minutes he saw Maggie emerge, and then the hotel manager, carrying Daniel in his car seat. Not even the image of another man carrying his son could break him out of the numb cold shell that was encasing his whole being.

Because the pain will kill you if you let it in.

He batted away the voice.

Nikos turned away from the window. And then he went straight back downstairs and into the casino. People looked up from the table, bleary-eyed.

'Ready for more, Marchetti?'

'Yes. Except this time I'm not playing for charity.'

One of the other men laughed. 'Does your wife know where you are?'

Nikos looked up, so cold and numb now that his voice felt as if it was coming from very far away. 'She doesn't matter. Let's get on with it.'

Maggie felt restless. She'd finished washing up the dishes in the sink and now she looked around the vast and gleaming kitchen which was situated in the basement of an even vaster house. A stunningly beautiful, period country house, to be exact. Set in some ten acres of lush green land about an hour's drive outside Dublin.

There were manicured gardens to the rear and a sizeable walled kitchen garden to the side. There was even a small lake and a forest.

And stables. But the stables were empty. Because the zillionaire heartless owner of the house couldn't even commit to a passing interest in racehorses, never mind an actual wife and baby—

Maggie put a hand to her belly, overcome with nausea for a moment. But then it passed and she drank some water.

She nursed her anger because it was the only thing that had got her through the last week and the headlines that screamed at her whenever she looked at anything online: *Honeymoon is over for Marchetti! Reformed Playboy no more! Is Marchetti back on the market?!*

It killed Maggie that she'd told him she loved him in a bid to try and get some reaction. A reaction he couldn't give because he was incapable. And the worst thing was he'd warned her all along.

At that moment she heard a sound from upstairs—the ground floor. A banging noise. The front door?

Maggie looked at the baby monitor on the table, Daniel was still asleep upstairs. She tucked the monitor into her back pocket and went upstairs. The knocker went again, louder, and she mut-

tered, 'Keep your hair on…' just as she switched
on the outside light and swung the door open.

And promptly ceased breathing at the sight in
front of her.

A tall dark man dominated the doorway, his
hand lifted as if to slam the knocker down again.
His other arm was raised and resting on the side
of the doorframe. The late-summer sky was a
dusky lavender behind him, making him seem
even darker.

Maggie couldn't find her breath. Dressed in
a classic black tuxedo, he was the most stupendously gorgeous man she'd ever seen. Thick, dark
curly hair and dark brows framed a strong-boned
face. Cheekbones to die for. Deep-set eyes, dark
but not brown. Slightly golden. His skin was dark.
There was stubble on his jaw.

His black bowtie hung rakishly undone under
the open top button of his shirt. Those dark eyes
flicked down from her face and moved over her
body—

She shook her head violently. *Déjà-vu*. This
had to be a particularly cruel and vivid form of
déjà-vu.

She opened her eyes. He was still there. Nikos
Marchetti. Her husband. Her ex-lover.

She'd known she'd have to see him again, but
not like this. She wasn't ready.

She turned and walked away from the front

door. 'You really should get a key cut to this house.'

'Ah, but would I be welcome?'

Maggie stopped and turned around. She hated it that she was even wearing almost exactly what she'd been wearing a year before. Cut-off denim shorts and a plaid shirt, tied at the waist. She'd spent the day cleaning the house, finding the monotonous work therapeutic.

Now she felt like a fool.

Once again Nikos was giving off an air of debauched hedonism, but she saw the way his sharp eyes moved over her. He was as sober as she was.

He frowned. 'Where's Mr Wilson?'

Maggie folded her arms. 'I gave him a few days off to visit his family.' And so she could lick her wounds in private.

She looked him up and down, trying to copy the way he looked at her—except she was probably failing dismally, because her gaze wanted to linger lovingly on every plane of his spectacular body.

'Were you at another function, shoring up the Marchetti brand?'

Or, worse, flirting with women? Her insides seized with pain.

'I was at a function in London, yes.'

Her heart thumped. He'd come all the way here straight from London?

'How's Daniel?'

Something inside her fell. She castigated herself. Of *course* this was about Daniel. He cared about his son. This was a *good* thing.

'He's fine—upstairs, asleep. If you want to talk about visitation rights I think it's best for all of us if we do it through intermediaries. This really isn't cool.'

He walked towards her, shucking off his jacket, letting it drop to the floor as he did so. He stopped in front of her. 'Oh, really? Intermediaries?'

Some of Maggie's bravado leached away. And some of the anger. Electricity crackled between them.

'Nikos…what's going on?'

For a second she thought he was going to kiss her, and then he stepped away and funnelled his hands through his hair. She could see the muscles in his back were taut. Of course he wasn't going to kiss her—he didn't want her. But then he turned around, eyes burning, and she was in his arms and his mouth was covering hers before she could form another thought.

Maggie's brain melted. And her bones. And her heart.

She clung to Nikos and he hauled her up against him. She wrapped her legs around him. His hands were under her bottom, holding her up.

She pulled back and sucked in air, heart hammering. He looked up at her. She pushed to get down and he released her.

She stepped back on trembling legs. 'What's going on? You said…you said desire faded…'

He emitted a bleak-sounding laugh. 'It was a lie. One of many.'

He reached for her hand with his. She looked at it warily.

He said, 'Please? Let me explain.'

She looked at him. Suddenly he didn't look so confident.

Against all her better instincts Maggie put her hand into his and let him lead her into the living room.

He let her go and walked over to the bookshelves. 'Your books are back.' He turned around. 'I missed them.'

'Nikos…'

She noticed then that he was unkempt. A bit wild. Dark circles under his eyes. Stubble. Actually, more than stubble. He looked as if he hadn't shaved in—

As if hearing her thoughts, he said, 'I don't think I've actually slept since you left last week. I went straight down to the casino and the whole week since has been a bit of a blur.'

Maggie felt anger rise again. 'I can show you the headlines if you want your memory refreshed. You fell out of the casino at lunchtime on—'

He held up a hand. 'I know.' He looked at her, deadly serious. 'But you see I was being an idiot. Because I love you. And when you said it to me

I couldn't believe it. I already felt guilty for infecting you with my toxicity, and—'

Maggie interrupted him. 'What did you just say?'

Nikos frowned. 'Which bit?'

She went over and caught his shirt in her hands and glared at him. 'You know *which bit*.'

He looked intense. More intense than she'd ever seen him.

'You did say you loved me didn't you? It wasn't a dream?'

She shook her head. 'Not a dream—reality. I do love you, Nikos. I think I fell in love with you that first moment I saw you. Tonight…just now… I thought I was dreaming you up…' A dam was breaking inside her.

Nikos caught her hands in his. His hands were shaking. He tugged her to sit down on the couch.

He looked down. 'You're still wearing your rings.'

Maggie flushed. 'I meant to take them off.'

He looked at her. 'I wouldn't blame you… I'm an idiot.'

'You've said that.'

'I love you.'

'You—?' She stopped. 'You really mean it?'

'Of course I love you… I just didn't know what I was feeling because I've never felt it before. But I remembered what you said about your mother… about doing anything for Daniel…and that's how I feel about you. And Daniel. I couldn't breathe this week, Maggie. I need you. I need you both. *So* much.' Then he said, 'Do you know why this is the only house I've ever bought?

She shook her head, reeling. Afraid to move in case she broke the spell.

He said, 'The first time I saw this house it appealed to something in me. I think I must have seen you here in a dream. And then I came and here you were. I've never had a home. Not a real, proper home. But when you opened that door something inside me went quiet for the first time in my life. I was *home*.'

He went on.

'I used to have panic attacks when I was at boarding school. They were brought on by a sense of being totally isolated and alone. I used to be sent home for the holidays with whichever poor unfortunate kid's family had offered to take me in. I didn't ever get to spend time with my own brothers. Sharif was abroad by then, building up his stake in the business. Maks was being shuttled between our father and his mother.'

Nikos's mouth twisted.

'They were no better off—I can see that now—but I imagined they were happier than me. I would watch the families I was with and feel toxic. I thought they must be able to see all the way into me, to where I was so jealous of them and the happiness they took for granted, and I vowed never to let myself want that. Because it felt like weakness. My own family didn't want me, so I obviously didn't deserve to be loved.'

Maggie reached out and cupped his jaw. 'Oh, Nikos...of *course* you deserved it. You deserved it more than anyone. You lost your mum so young...'

He pressed a kiss to her palm. 'I believed for a long time that she left me because I wasn't worth living for.'

'I can understand that. Especially when no one was around to tell you otherwise.'

'I've never let myself feel anything for anyone until you. It took me a year to come back to you.'

'You're here now.' Suddenly Maggie felt insecure. 'Are you sure? You're not just saying this because it's better for the company—?'

He was shaking his head. 'I would sell all my shares tomorrow if that would help convince you. I want us to have a home. A proper home. In Paris...here...wherever you want. My life is with you now, and with Daniel.'

Maggie felt ridiculously shy all of a sudden. 'I don't mind living in Paris or wherever. I just want a home with you and a safe, secure place for Daniel to grow and feel rooted. For our *family* to feel rooted.'

Maggie took his hand and put it on her belly.

He looked at her. 'You said...family?'

She nodded. 'I'm pregnant. Again. I was feeling nauseous... I didn't think it was possible... But apparently even if you're breastfeeding and

your periods haven't started again it's not impossible—'

Nikos pulled his hand away. 'Pregnant? Another baby?'

He stood up and left the room so abruptly that
she felt dizzy. She stood up too, her insides turning to jelly. It was too much. Too soon. Even the
strongest of relationships might not be able to cope
with a second pregnancy so soon after the first...

She waited to hear the sound of the front door
slamming but it didn't come.

Then Nikos reappeared in the doorway, with
a sleepy Daniel in his arms, his face wreathed
in smiles.

Maggie sat back down, her legs failing her.
Nikos came and sat down too. He held Daniel in
one arm and put his other hand on Maggie's belly.

'See here, *moro mou?* This is your little sister
or brother—right now, growing in Mama's belly.'

Maggie was crying now...sobbing. Nikos
reached for her and she wrapped her arms around
her husband and her baby, a joy such as she'd
never imagined possible filling every pore and
cell of her body.

After a long moment she pulled back, wiping
her eyes. 'I thought you...'

Nikos was shaking his head, and his eyes were
suspiciously shiny too. 'This has been my dream all
along too—I was just too scared to acknowledge it
to myself. Too scared to believe I might deserve it.'

'You *do* deserve it, my love.'

They kissed. Daniel gurgled. Maggie laughed through emotional tears.

Nikos said, 'Marry me again? Here? I want to give you a proper wedding day—to show you and everyone how much I love you.'

Maggie wiped at her tears and nodded and smiled. 'Yes, I'd like that.'

Seven months later. Spring. Ireland

Nikos and Maggie emerged from the small country church near Kildare House. Cherry blossoms had turned the ground pink and white. Nikos held his son Daniel high in one arm and his other arm was around his pregnant wife, stunning in a lace white dress, flowers in her long wavy hair.

Everyone cheered and clapped—and then started groaning when they kissed for an indecently long time.

When Nikos pulled back he looked down at his wife and said, 'Any regrets, Mrs Marchetti?'

She grinned. 'Never. Someone once told me that regrets were for losers.'

Two months later, in Paris, they welcomed their daughter Olympia—named after Nikos's mother—into the world.

An emotional Nikos introduced his son to his

little sister, and then he looked at Maggie on the bed, exhausted but happy. Never more beautiful.

She mouthed, *I love you*, and promptly fell asleep.

Nikos watched over his family as dawn broke outside on another beautiful day, and gave thanks for the woman who had opened his heart to love and shown him a world where not all sweetness was toxic.

* * * * *

If you fell in love with
The Maid's Best Kept Secret
Abby Green's 50th book for
Harlequin Presents
you're sure to adore these other stories
by the author!

Awakened by the Scarred Italian
Confessions of a Pregnant Cinderella
Redeemed by His Stolen Bride
The Greek's Unknown Bride

Available now